a Piece of Flotsam

Hilary Semmens

RAINBOWS PUBLISHING

Copyright © 1997 by Hilary Semmens

The right of Hilary Semmens to be identified as
Author of the Work has been asserted by her in accordance with the
Copyright, Designs and Patents Act 1988.

First published in Great Britain by Rainbows Publishing in 2004

All rights reserved. No part of this publication may be reproduced, stored
in a retrieval system, or transmitted, in any form or by any means
without the prior written permission of the copyright owner.

A catalogue record is available
for this title from the British Library

ISBN: 0 954823 50 8

Printed and bound in Great Britain by
Butler and Tanner
Burgess Hill
West Sussex

Rainbows Publishing
9 Atlantic Road South
Weston-Super-Mare
BS23 2DF

website
www.rainbows-publishing.co.uk

email
info@rainbows-publishing.co.uk

To Weston-super-Mare University of the Third Age

Chapter One

Stephen was evicted from under the pier at sundown, as 'this accommodation', so he was informed in savage hisses, was 'for ladies only'. He gathered his sleeping bag and backpack in his arms and backed out, apologising. Now that that their positions were reversed, what had been shapeless black figures against the sun were, he now saw, two hand-me-down valkyries in jumble sale reject couture, vivid in its level red light. The band stand, he discovered, was equally fiercely defended territory, this time by a man of indeterminate age, with matted dreadlocks and a rottweiler. The bus shelter in Beach Road was untenanted, but he soon found out why. Its seats were narrow sloping perches and its glass back did not so much divert the wind as focus it at ground level; no way could he lie there. He hunted along the front among the late-night remnants of the holiday crowds, settling eventually for the doorway of the derelict end-of-pier theatre. The sun was quite gone now and there, away from the loopy strings of lights that kept back the dark from the prom, a very few stars glimmered in the pale night sky of early June. At least he was out of the wind. He had not realised how cold it soon became after sunset, even, or perhaps especially, after so hot a day as it had been. Leaving home surfriding his rage and, still on an adrenalin high, entertaining friendly lorry drivers all the way to Weston with a torrent of speech, had been the easy bit - though what choice had he had? - but he had a lot to learn about being homeless. He pulled his sleeping bag tighter into his neck. He must get some sort of a job; there must be plenty of temporary work here with all the summer visitors. Maybe finding somewhere to live was more urgent. In any case, all being well and cross fingers, it was only until September, three months of summer weather. He slept.

Chapter Two

Alice never forgot the first time she saw Stephen. It was an incident she concealed, especially from Daphne, having no wish to boost that lady's belief in the supernatural, but even at the time the stranger's remark had come as a shock. 'He was on the rocks, that's the fact of the matter.' Startled, Alice had looked over her shoulder at the speaker, realised he was talking to someone else and looked back at the young fellow sitting on the pavement outside Boots who had caught her attention. For a moment her mind's eye filled with a picture of the youth spreadeagled on the rocks below her clifftop apartment. Dismissing the vision with an embarrassed shake of the head, she had chided herself for being over-imaginative. 'On the rocks,' for goodness sake! He appeared to be begging. Surely not, such a nicelooking boy. In this day and age. This was not Dickens's London. There were indeed all those articles in the Telegraph about homeless young persons, but this could not be one of them. Could he? Yet there it was - a red woollen cap with small change in it beside him, with a neat cardboard message, 'Homeless and hungry'. She knew better than to give to beggars; it must be right what that prime minister whose name one could never remember had said, that they are on the streets because they choose to be there. But it was such a sad young face, clean and fresh, with nicely combed hair. And what was that he was reading? Was it really Keats, her own special love? Standing there thinking in the midst of the crowds, right in someone's way, she found herself shouldered nearly to the ground, while the shopping throng drifted on oblivious. Only the beggar had got up with a look of concern. She waved him away with a little frightened twitch of a smile and a nod and he sank back.

That never-to-be-forgotten day it had been hot, a slow tide of grockles filling the High Street with all that over-exposed flesh of theirs glistening with perspiration and sun lotion. She savoured the word 'grockles', a delicious new name for holiday makers she had recently learned from her friend Nesta. The next time she was in town however, the fine weather had given way to grey swirls of rain that kept the trippers off, so that the street was uncrowded, if wet, and there he was again. He had squeezed even more tightly into the angle of Boots' portico, shrinking away from the sodden flaps of torn-off posters that floundered along the shop fronts, sheltering his book from the rain with his arm. The red cap was on his head, pulled over his ears. Poor bedraggled scrap, thought Alice.

"Whatever will you do when the weather gets really bad?" she said and then realised, abashed, that she had spoken out loud.

The boy looked up, blushed and struggled to his feet.

"I thought I would give you a pound," said Alice bravely, "but I don't know where to - what to..."

"You're very kind. Thank you," he replied, half uncurling his hand to take the coin, and managing to drop his book.

Her reflexes honed by years of caring for her aged parents, Alice stooped for it at the same time as he did and collided with him, recoiling sharply from the contact. His colour flamed as he drew back into wet-denimed untouchability.

"I didn't mean -" began Alice. Too late she understood that words are useless against insulting - what was it Nesta called it? - 'body language'. "Your poor book", she said, almost but not quite laying a placatory hand on his arm. "Is it very wet? Muddy? Oh dear." She found a tissue in her bag. "Keats, isn't it?"

He allowed her to take the book and wipe it as best she could.

"Keats is my favourite poet", she confided.

"Mine too, so far, but there's an awful lot of others I haven't read yet." He actually smiled.

She smiled back. "What is your name?"
"Stephen."
"Alice! Whatever are you doing?" Nesta Harbottle's

elocuted tones rang across the street. "You'll make yourself late. And that's not the half of it."

"Coming, Nesta." Alice was embarrassed. "Please excuse me. Stephen. - Oh, your book." She thrust it at him and scurried over to join her friends.

"Not giving him money, were you, honey?" asked Daphne. "Not wise, honestly."

"But he looks so hungry, poor boy."

"Buy him a bun and see what he does with it." Nesta's voice was the carrying kind. "Ditches it, pound to a penny. After money for something to stick into himself with a dirty needle, mark my words."

Alice darted a look at Stephen. There was no doubt he had heard. The pain twisting his face and the tears scuffed across it by his wet wrist etched themselves into her memory. She turned and bent her head into the rain, trotting along after the others.

This morning's meeting was in a big bare upstairs room of the Mermaid Tavern. They had to go in through the bar, a real experience for Alice, whose parents had disapproved of public houses. Its usefulness as a community facility and the geniality of its atmosphere were among many revelations she had had of late. When her mother had died the previous autumn in her hundredth year, outliving her father by twenty five years but, alas, not quite making it to the Queen's telegram, she had sold the family home and taken a flat in the resort she remembered from her early childhood when the family still took holidays. A welcoming neighbour had invited her to join the University of the Third Age (U3A) and she had entered it as through a long-shut door into a brave new world. It had 'such people in it', open-hearted, open-minded people, without whom she would have found it terrifying, but, clutching at helping hands as she went, she was finding her way round the nineties just in time to leave them, delighted by unexpected insights into problems so deeply knotted into the seventy years of her personal history that she hardly knew they were there.

"What's so funny?" demanded Nesta.

Alice doused her private smile. "Nothing", she said. She

was afraid if Nesta knew she thought it was ironic for a Salvation Army captain to address a social philosophy group in a pub, there would be po-faced explanations of how it was precisely because of the Movement's Victorian anti-drinking crusade that much of their work had been done in such places and martyrs made there to boot. She could almost hear Nesta's pedagogic tones. The smile crept back.

Captain Gilford was a mine of information. He told them the why and the where and the who of his organisation past and present, the importance of the music ('so that the devil doesn't have all the best tunes') and the quaint uniform ('Everyone knows who we are and what we're up to'), the pitfalls of large scale finance that beset the most innocent of the unwary in what was inevitably a large financial enterprise. Alice began to shift her thinly upholstered pelvis on the plastic chair seat. There was no coffee break during these meetings; the landlord banked on recouping the costs of lending the room (lit, however dimly, and warmed in the cold weather by cumbersome, creaking radiators) by selling them all refreshments at the bar before and after the meeting. Alice meditated wistfully upon the cosy cup of coffee she had shared with Mr. Ratcliffe the other day. No smeary windows and nicotine-stained wallpaper in that bright little coffee shop, its glowing dark wood walls hung with twinkling plates. What a nice man Mr. Ratcliffe was, poor soul, all alone after looking after his little dotty wife all those years. It must have been so difficult for him with his dreadful arthritis, or whatever it was that had confined him to that very superior wheelchair. So much worse than it had been for her with dear Mummy and Daddy, blessed as she had always been with such wonderful health. Really the poor man could do with a little looking after himself. Alice blushed to remember how suspicious she had been of him when he had first accosted her in the Italian Gardens, so kindly defending her from that rude woman with the little girl. Why should she not speak to a child? She had thought she was lost, as indeed the little soul had believed herself to be, poor lamb. A strange world where one could be blamed for trying to comfort a distraught child. How comforting it had been to have his support. A kind man and certainly a gentleman; she had ventured to trust herself to a second meeting with him, doubtful as she was about what Mummy would have said. She would like to reciprocate his kindness in some small way. But he was so independent, what Daddy would have called 'a man of vigorous mind'. Not that that was necessarily a compliment in Alice's view; Father always seemed to her to admire rather ruthless characters, clearsighted and resolute, regardless of the feelings of weaker souls, Kipling's sort of men. Mr. Ratcliffe was not like that, she thought, strong, yes, but very considerate. What would he have said had he seen that little encounter with the boy Stephen, she wondered. He would surely never have insulted the unfortunate young fellow as Nesta and Daphne had. Poor boy, there must be a story behind his plight.

Once again Alice took herself aback by voicing her next thought aloud, her voice cutting though the restless susurration accompanying the captain's discourse and stopping him in full statistical flow.

"What do you know about the homeless in this town Captain Gilford? Are they really all worthless vagabonds?"

For a moment the man's jaw hung open. Then he bent a brightened eye on Alice, face and posture suddenly alive. "Certainly not, madam. Some are, of course. They're a varied bunch, like the rest of us. There are many reasons for them being there. They are my friends, I know them all."

All eyes were focussed on the captain now, some sceptical, some curious, some sentimental, all polite and attentive.

"I regard it as part of my job to keep an eye on them," he went on, heartened by the changed atmosphere. "We serve supper in the Citadel four nights a weeks - I wish it could be more - we desperately need volunteers, ladies and gentlemen, as well as funds - and I make it my business to check on my regulars if they don't show up."

"How do you do that then?" barked Len, the retired postmaster. "By definition, no doors to knock on."

"We are all creatures of habit, sir, and think of one place as our own, even if it's only a corner of a multistorey car park or a spot under an archway out of the wind. There are two elderly ladies who have slept by the sea wall under the pier for three months of every year since I've been here."

"Ladies?" exploded Nesta.

"On their holidays I suppose," commented Daphne facetiously.

The captain gave her a straight look.

"Precisely, madam," he said. "These friends of mine do not have an address, but I assure you they have the same wants and desires as ourselves and that they do settle on a place of abode, if not a fixed one, even if only fleetingly. The other evening, for example, I found one particular sea front shelter vacant on my goodnight round. Next day I chanced upon its usual occupant on the High Street and commented on the absence. 'Sorry brother', he said, 'I'd been visiting friends and got home very late.' You see?"

"'Home'! How touching!" Elsie from the drama group had on her Christmas story face.

"Poor fellow -"

"Women too. I didn't realise."

"Don't you remember Edna the Inebriate Woman? 'I am not the vagrant!' Wonderful play."

"Patricia Hayes - marvellous actress - wasted for so long in those rubbishy -"

Nesta's voice recalled them all like a battle field bugle: "The afflicted elderly must of course have proper care, but, no patience with these young dropouts. Parasites. All starts with lager and glue-sniffing behind the bike sheds. Seen it all. Professionally. Ends up whingeing beggary and dirty needles. Mugging us old women in the streets, smashing up our homes. All to get the next fix."

Alice stared at her, her face fine-pleated with worry. Was this her friend speaking? Who had been such a trojan for her when she first moved down here in the wake of her bereavement, though she had only met her in the corner shop? Could she possibly be right. Was this what she saw when she looked at Stephen? Had she really looked at him at all? Perhaps - probably - the captain knew Stephen. She must ask him, see what he thought.

Captain Gilford was winding up. David, the chairman, once head teacher of a large school, was thanking him with wit and grace and flagging the next meeting's topic. Alice clapped along with the rest and then sought among the damp aromatic mass of rainwear for her mac.

"Madam."

She jumped like a pony at a firework, to find the captain at her elbow.

"So sorry to make you jump," he said. "I just wanted to thank you for opening things up as you did. It's a lesson I'll take on board for the future."

"I am afraid I am rather troubled," she confessed as he helped her on with her mac. She had not noticed before how young and fresh-faced the man was. "Some of the nicest people's reactions seem so exceedingly unkind. I wonder if you - I expect you have come across a boy called Stephen..."

But David had swept the captain away with an (unaccepted) invitation to a pub lunch.

Alice slipped out. She was in no mood for Nesta and Daphne's moral certitudes for the walk back. The wind and rain had died away, so she put her wet rain hood into her pocket. Conspicuously crowned with white curls, her erect little figure bobbed briskly across the near-deserted Grove Park. Half a dozen young lads were idly kicking a ball about, all of them wearing baseball caps, jeans and trainers and identical T shirts with a flamboyant black and purple design. Alice was trying discreetly to make out what it represented.

"Right! Go go go!" cried one of them and, to her astonishment they converged on her in a rush, giggling and panting, jostling and spinning her till she fell half into a flower bed. As suddenly as they had come they were gone. And so was her bag. She sat up, legs all askew, staring at her muddy hands and sleeves in amaze. She tried to wipe off some of the mud on the grass, but without success because she had begun to shake so much. A constriction in her chest hunched her over till her face bowed nearly to the ground, tears dripping from nose and cheeks to mingle with the raindrops lingering there.

"You all right, Miss? They hurt you?" Stephen's soft voice was close to her ear. She shook her head, with a muffled squeak that was meant to be a reassuring negative.

"Here's your bag. They threw it away when they'd taken your purse out of it. I'm sorry about that."

"It doesn't matter," she said, smearing her pocket, her handkerchief and then her face with mud before she realised what she was doing. "That only had credit cards in it. I can stop those. And a tiddly bit of change. As long as they did not think to look in the flap in the bag where my real money is."

"They didn't." Stephen's smile was the more delightful for its rarity. "How they missed those notes I don't know - sticking halfway out when I picked up the bag they were. Too excited I guess. To be honest I doubt whether they'd ever done anything like this before. They're only silly kids. Here, let's get you off this wet ground. Can you stand?"

Leaning on his slight frame, she clambered to her feet.

"All right?" he asked. "Do you want an ambulance or anything? Shall I get the police?"

"Oh no no no. There is no need for any fuss. I may ring the police when I get home." She took a step and faltered. "It would be very kind of you to walk me there. I do in fact not feel quite the thing."

"No problem. It's shock. Are you sure you don't need an ambulance? Or I could get you a cab?"

"No thank you. I shall do very well. It is not far. Then perhaps you would like to join me for some lunch."

He saw her safely home, but refused to come in for lunch or even for a wash. "I'm not fit to come in a house", he said. "There's a place where I wash in the Sovereign Centre toilets." But he did bashfully accept one of the notes he had salvaged and lurked out of sight down the side alley while she made him a sandwich. She watched from the window as he went off with it towards the sea front. So sad, she thought, such a caring boy. And loves Keats. What had brought him to this? And where was his 'place of abode'? And how 'fleeting' was his sojourn there?

Oh dear, she had not even thanked him properly.

Chapter Three

"Did I do right, do you think?"

Alice was having coffee with Mr. Ratcliffe in the rose garden behind the Rose Tea Rooms. The hot weather was back, ladling the opulent scent of the Guiné rose over them from the arched trellis under which they sat. Mr. Ratcliffe looked at the earnest little wrinkled face beneath her big straw hat and smiled.

"I'm sure you did. We don't want to drive these kids into a life of crime by giving them a premature criminal record, but it doesn't do to let them think they've got away with it or they get the message it's OK to do more outrageous things."

"I really didn't want them punished, you know. Stephen assured me it must have been their first experiment with crime. It is not as though they did me much harm in the end."

"And they were not punished, unless you call a good telling off by the sergeant punishment. You never know, if they're basically decent lads it may just have done the trick."

"I do hope so." Alice sighed. Her gaze wandered to the ancient Mermaid rose spreading wide its cream and honey blooms on the wall. There are some things that, fragile as they may seem, go on down the decades even through these disconcerting times. She sipped her coffee. The Rose did coffee properly, in little individual cafetières. Mr. Ratcliffe said it reminded him of Italy. She had not expressed her stay-at-home preference for a freeze-dried version, but she did enjoy the tiny almond confections that came instead of biscuits. She could tell him that.

"Clever boy, that Stephen of yours," he said. "Have you run into him since?"

"I'm afraid not." She bit her lip. "The U3A has stopped for the summer and I do my shopping early nowadays to avoid the trippers, so I am never in town when he is likely to be there. I ought to make a point of it though. He was so kind. I wish there was something I could do for him, poor child. What do you think? I cannot determine what to do for the best."

"Then ask him," said Mr. Ratcliffe. "Would he be there now, do you suppose? I'd come and give you moral support, but me rolling up in this buggy of mine might be making too much of an issue of it."

Alice blinked and squared herself up. "You are right, of course. I shall go straight away." She turned an appealing face to him. "Would you ...?"

He saw her to the entrance to the High Street. She peered through the drifting crowds, not so thick today; the tide being just right, the families were all on the beach. There the boy was, crouched against Boots as ever. She gave her escort a little wave and set off.

"Stephen."

He jumped and got to his feet. "Morning, Miss. How're you doing?"

"I am very well, thank you, Stephen. Oh, what is that you have there? Not Keats today?"

"No, Kerouac. He was a beat writer, bummed his way across America."

"Like W.H.Davies?"

"Who?"

"You must have heard of him. He is, after all, a modern poet and another of my favourites. 'What is this life, if, full of care,/We have no time to stand and stare/To lean upon a gate and browse/And stare as long as sheep and cows.'"

"I'm sorry?"

"Oh, what am I thinking?" cried Alice in confusion. "True, he appears in the Oxford Book of Modern Verse but that came out before the war, while I was at school. He must be very old hat to you in fact."

"Sorry?"

"Oh dear, I mean, not modern at all. Davies's Autobiography of a Super Tramp came out even before the other war, the Great War, nearly a hundred years ago, when my father was about your age."

15

"Oh." He nodded politely.

She made the venture. "Stephen, I am worried about you." He threw her a sidelong glance, animal-like, but she tucked her chin down and went on. "I could give you a little more money - no, you are not to interrupt - but I am not in a position to give you much and in any case that does not address your problem - whatever that is, and I am certainly not prying. However, if there were something I could do to help? You know you cannot go on like this."

"I don't intend to go on like this." He turned his flaming face away with an angry lift of his chin. "I have plans." He drooped again. "Well, hopes. But I don't know how..."

"How what, Stephen?" That momentary look of arrogance had disturbed her, but the expression he turned towards her now was diffident, childlike.

"Miss, if you would really like to help me, there is something. It would really save my ar-" He flushed at the word he had been going to use and with a sidelong look at her said 'save me' instead. "It's with me not having an address. I hadn't foreseen that. I can write to my mother, you see, but she can't write back."

"Oh Stephen, of course, you have a mother! How stupid of me - I never thought! Oh, the poor soul, not knowing where you are! She must be worried to death -" Alice stopped in midsentence to look at his again half-averted face. His chin was quivering. She put a tentative hand on his arm. "I'm so sorry," she whispered. "I do not intend to be rude and pry. But if there is any way in which I can help, please tell me."

"If it isn't too cheeky" - he bent his head and earnestly examined his frayed and grubby cuffs. "There is something. Could you let me give her your address? I really need my A-level results and they'll be sent to me at home, so she'll have them -"

"A-level results? My dear boy!" She fumbled in her bag for a biro and a page from her diary. "Better still - excuse me" –
She disappeared into Smiths, returning after a gnawing interval with a writing pad, two large envelopes and a couple of stamps.

"Here you are. You can put in an s.a.e. No, what use is that? Come along and we will find a table where you can write. - No, no need to fret. I shall not take you anywhere where you might feel uncomfortable. The place is well tucked away in a garden."

Mr. Ratcliffe was in his buggy at the corner still, patiently awaiting her return. She introduced them.

"He needs to write to his mother. To obtain his A-level results! What do you think of that! Oh Stephen, I do hope you get good news."

"Might as well all have some lunch." Mr. Ratcliffe turned his wheelchair around. "You can do your letter while we're waiting for the food to arrive."

They made their way back down the narrow alley, full of the smells of sea breeze-seasoned cooking. No-one had come into the rose garden since they had left. Mr. Ratcliffe motioned the boy to a shady table and he and Alice returned to the one that had so recently been theirs. He gave their order, salad for Alice and steak pie and vegetables for himself and Stephen. As he bent his head to write they watched him. So young he was, so very young. A tendril of hair lay in the hollow of his nape. It seemed to reach out, sweet pea-like, and twine itself into her spinsterly heart. His clothes had become quite dreadful, but his person was as clean as a primrose and as sweet; she was suddenly aware of the pathos, and the courage, of those ablutions in the Sovereign Centre toilets.

"Could be my grandson," murmured Mr. Ratcliffe.

Alice looked at him, startled. She had heard about his wife's pitiful illness, but nothing of their younger selves.

"You have grandchildren?"

"Two. In Massachusetts, alas. Haven't seen them in years. Kennan, the eldest, did come over with my son and daughter-in-law for his grandmother's funeral, but I can't honestly say my memory of that time is any too clear."

"Would it be possible for you to make the journey to see them?" Alice glanced at the electric buggy and his two clinical-looking sticks. Family was so important. Now Mummy and Daddy were both gone, she had none. The airlines made special arrangements for disabled people, did they not?

Stephen put stamps on both the envelopes, folded his letter and tucked it into one of them. Then he joined them at their table.

"Would you please put your name and address on this

other envelope so Mum can send it back?"

She complied. Mr.Ratcliffe's eye strayed to the first envelope, making out the address upsidedown. Thought I recognised the accent, he told himself smugly. Their lunch arrived.

"This is brilliant of you," said Stephen, sealing the second envelope inside the first with the letter and pocketing it. He was transformed, bright and lively and full of smiles. It was hardly true to say that up to that point he had always looked haggard, like Keats's knight-at-arms, thought Alice, but, oh, so woebegone. His table manners were quite respectable, she observed, with slightly shamefaced approval, not quite the Ritz perhaps, though heaven knew, the people who apparently frequented the Ritz these days. Not that she had ever done so herself; she had learned her etiquette from Mother. There was no question, however, that he appreciated his food. And always so polite.

"Stephen's reading a modern poet today, aren't you, Stephen. Tell Mr. Ratcliffe who it is. I fear I have forgotten."

"He's not quite what you would call a poet, Miss, more of an autobiographical novellist, Jack Kerouac. 'Spontaneous prose', he called it. And not exactly modern, said of himself he was 'one of the crazy illuminated hipsters of the beat generation'. Died some time back in the sixties, I think."

Alice blinked and smiled uncertainly.

"On The Road, is it?" queried Mr. Ratcliffe. "Yes, I see it is. English Lit. one of the A-level results you're waiting for?"

"Yes, sir. Eng. Lit. and Lang., Psychology and Spanish. And Latin GCSE. I thought Spanish would be useful in South America and I guess if you have Spanish Portuguese is pretty much a doddle to pick up."

"South America?"

"Oh, my mind's been set on travelling for a long time, sir. Backpacking of course. Especially South and Central America. Borges and Gabriel Garcia Marquez, all those."

Alice had not seen him like this before, so sparkling with energy.

"And how do you plan to do that, young man?" Mr.Ratcliffe was twinkling kindly at him.

Stephen looked at him sharply and straightened up. "Ah,

well, if all goes to plan, I'll have to work dead hard for the next three years, maybe more, but then -"

"So you do have a plan. But you're hardly what one might call working now, are you, let alone 'dead hard'?"

"No sir. But this is a learning experience. Look at the use Kerouac made of his bad times and that guy - what was it again, Miss? - who stared at cows. And this" - he waved his hand vaguely - "is strictly temporary."

"There are temporary jobs, especially in a seaside town like this. There's no need to beg."

Stephen's ready colour flooded up. Oh dear, thought Alice, don't destroy him just when his spirits are reviving. But the boy was not going to be faced down.

"That's what I thought when I came here, but, sir, you try finding a job, any job at all, if you haven't got an address."

"Fair enough. But how and when do you propose to put that right?"

Alice was twisting her hands.

Stephen's angry chin went up again. "Sir, I have plans, real plans, if you don't mind."

"All depending on those A-levels I suppose?"

"Yes, sir."

"And it's none of my business?"

"Well... No sir."

"And you don't want to tempt fate by telling us?"

A grin mercifully dissipated that arrogant expression. "That's about it, sir."

How proud he is, thought Alice. Aloud she said, "You must know Captain Gilford, Stephen?"

"The Sally Army man," put in Mr.Ratcliffe. "Does a lot of good for chaps down on their luck I believe."

The sneering look returned. "That happy-clappy bible-basher? No thank you. He does my head in. Bloody know-all do-gooders. Beg your pardon Miss, but..."

Alice broke a long silence. "I try to do good, Stephen," she said humbly.

He turned convulsively towards her, his face working, near tears. "Oh Miss, you do, you do do good. You're the kindest

person I've ever met. You don't poke your nose in -"
(One in the eye for me, thought the man.)
"- or patronise me -"
(And one for the Sally Army fellow.)
"- you truly listen and make me feel it matters what I think and what I do with my life."
(And a deserved bouquet for you, old girl.)
The waitress arrived.
"Pudding, anyone?" asked Mr. Ratcliffe. "No? All full up? Coffee then?"
Harmony and better than that was restored over coffee. Mr. Ratcliffe, it transpired, knew a lot about the Americas, having forayed widely on business trips. His job had been establishing agricultural machinery factories all over the world for his engineering firm, so he had had to establish working relationships with all sorts and conditions of men in exotic places and languages. The boy was as full of eager questions as the man was happy to satisfy them. Alice listened in rapt wonder. The girl came with the bill and Mr. Racliffe paid it.
"Time to post your letter, young man. There's a box on the corner. No - no need for thanks. I've been thoroughly enjoying myself. Good luck with those results and here's to Spanish America."
They left the garden with him and watched him kiss the envelope before dropping it through the slot, then stood together a moment looking down over the beach and across the languid sea. Suddenly the boy jumped up on to the sea wall, poised with arms flung wide and head back in exultation.
"Yeeeoowwww" he cried, turned like a dancer and ran a few yards along the top of the wall before leaping down and running, running and leaping until they could see him no more.
"Bless you, dear," murmured Alice, not sure which of them she meant. "What a treat it is to see him looking so gay and carefree."
He gazed at her fondly and she blushed. The twitch at the corner of his mouth caught her eye.
"Oh, Mr. Ratcliffe, how silly of me. I forgot that was one of the good old words one can no longer use, or so my friend Nesta

20

tells me. He would not have been pleased to hear me call him that, would he."

"Probably not, though you never can tell. And what's with all this 'Mr. Ratcliffe' eh'? Very oldfashioned between friends. Went out in the fifties I believe."

"Ah, but you see," she said, laughing, "I am very old-fashioned. But, Peter, I shall be very glad to call you my friend."

Chapter Four

Alice bought two quiches for the price of one at Tesco's and gave one to Stephen. They ate them sitting quietly together in the Italian Gardens.

"If I don't hear soon it'll be too late," he said, breaking the silence, his voice harsh with self control.

"Why, Stephen, why? How do you mean it will be too late?"

"It'll be too late, that's all. It's been a fortnight already. That's me, finished."

"Stephen, you cannot say that. You must not. Perhaps your letter went astray. These things do happen, you know." She could only remember a single instance in the whole of her life (an important business letter during her brief reign as her father's personal secretary, a painful memory) but all the same, she thought. "Suppose we try again."

He did meet her eye for a flickering moment. "I'm afraid I kept your paper and Mr. Ratcliffe's biro and used it all up. I'm sorry."

"There is no need to be. They were meant for you. How did you manage for stamps?"

"Oh, not letters. Other things."

"Diaries? Things like that?"

"Yeah." He was avoiding her questioning look.

"If I were a betting man, as Mr. Ratcliffe would say, I'd wager you were writing poetry."

He shrugged and drooped lower, hardly stirring when she trotted off to Smiths for further supplies of stationery and stamps, but achieving a grin and a bracing of the shoulders on her return. "You're right of course, Miss." This time there was none of the exultancy of expectation as he wrote and dutifully posted his letter. Watching him, Alice's own face crumpled with pain.

"Here's some money, Stephen," she said. "I am unlikely to have so much free time for a while. The U3A term has begun. But I will make sure you get your answer as soon as it arrives."

"Don't worry, Miss. You could signal me from your window if you like. What time does the post come?"

And so it was arranged. She longed to know in what way the results were to be the open-sesame to a new life, but could not bring herself to quiz him. Peter might well have found out, but he was away in Sheffield visiting his other son and daughter-in-law, who had no children and both worked in the new university there. Alice was disconcerted to realise that she was lonely without him, in spite of her U3A commitments and all the friends she had made thereby. She told herself that to make herself busy all day was the best thing she could do. It was pointless to brood over Stephen's predicament. If he felt himself unable to confide in her she could not even begin to address his problems. She looked at his shuttered face and stoic posture, forearms limp across his knees, the biro and notepad hanging dead in his hands. Well, at least the letter had gone, a positive step had been taken. Fruitless worrying would help no-one.

It was time to leave for her History Group meeting. She stood up, her troubled eyes still upon him, sitting there like one of the pieces of bric-a-brac slowly turning to stone under the drips of Mother Shipton's petrifying well. They had seen that during their wonderful holiday in Yorkshire, Daddy's retirement holiday, how many years - decades - ago now? There had been no holidays since; Mummy had not been well enough. With a glint of mischief she made up her mind. She was under no obligation to go to the group. She would play truant for the first time in her life. If you undertake to do something, her father had said, if you put your hand to the plough, you must never turn back, 'muck or nettles' as the foreman had so quaintly put it. But no-one would be any the worse if she missed this meeting. They would entertain themselves for a minute wondering about her absence, that was all. With a thrill of wickedness she snapped the last thread of conscience.

"Shall we go out in the car, Stephen?" she cried.

"Stephen, will you come out for a drive with me? Why not? It would be fun, Stephen, would it not?"

He shook himself alert and looked up at her. "What? Oh, a drive? You got a car then, Miss?"

"Yes indeed. I hardly ever use it since I moved here. I had it when Mother was alive, to take her to the doctor and the hospital and shopping, things like that. But here I am within walking distance of everywhere I want to go. We could go into the country or down the coast. We could see a bit of the world." A memory of wild rides in the dickey seat of Daddy's old Morris arose and turned itself into a fond smile - wild rides to her, that is, and from today's standards highly dangerous, a small child tucked in a rug unrestrained in the open back of the car, the dickey, like an open boot indeed, but to her careful elderly father the picture of family decorum. "You'd like that, wouldn't you? It would be spiffing, would it not?" She was still thinking of her father. "Would it not, Stephen?"

He stood up, his back to her, his neck and shoulders working as if he were throwing her off.

"Oh, for God's sake! I'm not a little kid!"

Humbled, she went to her meeting, though her mind was not on it.

"Penny for 'em," said Nesta as they parted afterwards. "Never do say much anyway. Be nice if you could look interested though." Nesta was the leader of that group.

"I'm sorry, Nesta," said Alice, "I truly am. I am worried about something, I do confess. Yes indeed. And no, it is really not something you can help me with, I fear."

The idea of driving once planted, she went down to her garage at the end of the block a morning or so later to get her Mini out and of course it failed to start. So much for taking the boy for a spin. Maybe he would have taken over, manlike, and that might have cheered him up, she thought wryly. The RAC came in less than an hour and got her on the road, a 'jump start' they called it, and sent her off for a twenty mile drive to charge the battery, with a recommendation to consult her garage about a new one. While they were working she checked her documents and found to her horror that she had nearly outrun her MOT. More problems to exercise her during those twenty miles along the byways, dutiful, not 'spiffing' at all, and reminding her all the way how easy it is to get out of practice and lose confidence. Use it or lose it, she chided herself, echoing Nesta. She must drive more or get rid of the car altogether. Would she get anything for a thirty year old Mini, she wondered. Either way it must be put in order, so she arranged to take it into a garage the following day.

The mechanic estimated about an hour's work, so there was time for a walk in the unfamiliar downtown area, strung out with cash-and-carries, DIY stores and so forth looming like beached whales in windy parking acres, with bald roads designed for cars and lorries, where to proceed on foot was to be an alien, unable to relate to the environment in any human way. Alice walked a brisk mile and paused on a bridge to look at the railway beneath. There were people laughing and scuffling right under where she stood. Someone kicked a can, which went rattling and clinking among the echoes. They must be under the bridge, right beside the track. She tried to picture how much space there was there, how much headroom, what it would be like when the trains came through. Other feet were coming crunching along the clinker of the verge on the far side of the bridge behind her.

A voice cut through, clear and authoritative. "What do you think you're doing? That's private property. Put it back."

There was an abrupt hush.

She could not possibly be mistaken. It was Stephen's voice. Peter had been right that he must have been a good prefect, if not head boy.

"Wurrrhhh!" A crowing jeer ruptured the silence. "Who says? You? Poof!"

A chorus of indistinguishable adolescent voices, bassoon-deep to fife screech, out of tune and harsh, filled the resonant space beneath her feet.

"Poof! Poof! - Where's your daddy then? - This stuff yours then? - Hiding your dirty washing in a hole in the wall? - Who's a litter lout then? - Naughty naughty - load a junk - that's pollution that is - tell you what, save you a trip, we'll take it down the tip for you, eh? - Poof! Poof!"

A rabble of boys, dressed - she might have known it - in

black and purple T shirts and baseball caps, burst into sight, squealing with glee. They ran a little way up the track, unbundling a sleeping bag as they went, ripping it, shaking things out of a towel, tossing books into the air, tussling over them, tearing them, making fountains of scraps of paper from notepaper pads. As Alice watched in helpless disbelief, a gust of wind whirled the pages away in a squandering spiral. A couple of sheets writhed in an updraught and sideslipped over the parapet into a puddle at her feet. Quickly she picked them up and blotted the worst of the water away with her handkerchief. By the time she straightened up the gang was in triumphant flight, the desecrated sleeping bag abandoned.

Stephen emerged, moving like an old man, to retrieve such of his belongings as he could. She yearned to call out to him and offer comfort, but she couldn't. What was he to do now? Was the underside of this bleak bridge what Captain Gilford would term his 'place of abode'? How dreadful. And now these wretched boys had discovered it, where would he go? Was his sleeping bag quite ruined? Autumn was upon them; would he not be terribly cold? Come the winter, would he not get hypothermia and die? Oh, he must not! Surely these plans of his would come to fruition in time. Whatever they were.

As he went about his pitiful salvage, oblivious to her on his skyline, Alice stood there dumb. She recognised that he had been hurt enough already; knowing that she had been a witness to his humiliation would be past all bearing. What could she do? She had a put-u-up settee in her flat. Ought she to offer him a home? How would he respond? Would he simply be driven away completely? If the worst came to the worst he would have to swallow his pride in order to save his life. Perhaps she could adopt him. What would Peter say? But she was forgetting his mother - did he have a father? She really could not come to terms with the contemporary dysfunctional family. If that was what his was. She had never come across one herself as far as she knew, but there were endless discussions of them in the Telegraph.

He had assembled the wrack of his belongings now and was trudging away towards the station. He must never know what she had seen, she understood that, but then how could she help him? She could let him have a new toothbrush and so forth without giving anything away, but inevitably a minefield of potential misapprehensions had been laid between them. Even if she had not already forfeited ... 'Oh, for God's sake, Miss, I'm not a little kid.'

He was out of sight now. She remembered the soggy pages in her hand and bent her head to decipher what was left of the writing.

> *My coloured dust sheet over the stars was fusty and cumbrous...*

Had he really written that himself, out of his head? Not that she was any judge, but to her it sounded like real poetry. What did it mean? Rather more had survived on the other sheet.

> *Oh my dear,*
> *What shall I be this time next year?*
> *Too near for sight or too far or clear*
> *In this two-dimensional weave and sway*
> *Shadowless interplay*
> *Colour and sound surface unbroken within*
> *my sphere?*

Then water had filled the crease across the middle of the page and some lines were obliterated.

> *One after one you the ember-eyed dreams*
> *Move on the sphere surface unreachable*
> *though your hearts beat warm to my arms,*
> *Though I strive as buds in the morning strain against the white*
> *Sky curvilinearly bounding them with a margin of lig...*
> *Too far for swimming to the underwater sta...*
> *Altogether too fa...*
> *One af....ne...*

Alice could not make out any more. Half-blinded with tears, she blundered back to pick up her car.

Chapter Five

Nesta Harbottle came up to Alice's flat for a coffee before taking her and Daphne Spriggs out to visit one of the local National Trust properties. This was always a pleasure for her. She loved the view from the windows; the curving westward coastline, hills beyond hills, headlands beyond headlands, indistinguishable in the end - on a day like this one - from lines of shimmering azure clouds; the sea, armour-plated in silver now, never the same; the deep rocky cove directly below.

"Ghastly when the southwesters come powering in no doubt," she said, then, recoiling from the taste of sour grapes, qualified the thrust of the remark. "Damn solid building, whatever. Victorians knew how to make the well-heeled comfortable." She sat back and cast an appreciative eye round the ornate cornices and clustered ceiling rose. "Great place, this. Don't know your luck." Her own flat did have a squinting view over Grove Park, but it was a fourth floor box in a fifties block and the balcony was no longer safe. She had been obliged to get rid of so many books and bits of furniture when the house had to be sold after Ed died. She hadn't realised he would leave her with so little to live on. If they had had children, if only, she would arguably not have been reduced to living in a crumbling cupboard, a lonely old bat cuddling up to other lonely old bats for company. Steady the Buffs, no if-onlies, she told herself sharply. Be grateful you've still got the pesky Peugeot and the wherewithal, just, to run it.

Daphne arrived. "That boy's there again," she said, taking off her jacket and settling down by the window. With a guilty start Alice hurried from the kitchen to the landing window. He was on the other side of the road, looking up, springing into alertness when he saw her. She gave him a sad smile and a rueful shake of the head. Hope deferred maketh the heart sick, she sighed to herself, as his head drooped and he shambled away down the road. It was almost October now; a fortnight had gone by since the posting of the second letter. How could his mother not...? It was pitiful beyond belief. She had only seen him once face to face since the bridge incident. Then she had given him a toilet bag with tooth things, a face cloth and soap in a box, mumbling something about these things not lasting for ever, and the boy had been polite but noncommittal. Conversation had been strained and awkward. Both were glad of her need to get away for her social philosophy meeting.

The kettle boiled, recalling her to her duties.

"Seen off your stalker?" asked Daphne, accepting her cup.

"Amounts to harassment, Alice. Asked for it though. Need your head testing for letting him find out where you live. 'Walking you home'! Tuh!"

"Really Nesta, I told you quite clearly how that came about and how well he behaved." Nesta, once a further education lecturer, would surely have understood about the examination results, but Alice had scruples about divulging what had been confided in so intimate and, at the time, so joyful a setting. It was none of her business. And an overarching sense of dread was beginning to loom above - no, she must not - What was it Peter had said about tempting fate?

Nesta's voice interrupted her thought. "Masterminded the whole set-up, mark my words. Boy like that. Manipulate that little gang no problem."

"Oh Nesta! He and those boys are poles apart. How could you say such a thing? You know it is absolute crap."

Her two guests exploded into laughter.

"I love you, Alice," said Daphne, wiping her eyes.

"Why? What's so funny?"

"What you just said, dear. So out of character. I bet you don't know what it means."

"Of course I do. It is an alternative and even stronger expression for 'utter nonsense'. You say it all the time, Nesta."

"Well, don't you say it? We know when we can and when we can't. Look it up in the dictionary."

Alice sighed. She had done it again. Oh the pitfalls for the unwary in this brave new world - language, language, 'Gay' she had already learned not to say, and 'knockers', though she was still not sure why, such a pity to lose useful words like that.

They thoroughly enjoyed their day out. Alice had visited the house years before when Father still took pleasure in going out in the car, but this was so different. They had lunch in the stables restaurant, a deliciously wicked extravagance; homemade soup and crusty bread followed by syllabub, served by girls in mob caps and big aprons, instead of the kind of picnic meal she used to prepare for her parents and herself and serve on paper plates and linen napkins on the most secluded bench they could find. Nesta's knowledgeableness and Daphne's irreverence brought the place so much more alive than 'getting one's money out of the guide book' had done. Remembering how lovely the grounds had been when she had come with these friends in May, she had expected them to be past their best now, but the sprawling wealth of autumn growth enraptured her.

Bouncing home along the lanes in Nesta's Peugeot, invigorated and content, they came within sight of the sea just as the lowering sun turned it to honey.

"Drop me at the end of your road, Nesta, if you please. I love walking up on an evening like this. It has been such a wonderful day. Thank you so much."

"Pleasure, Alice," beamed Nesta. "Caught the sun, what! Alice the rednosed - well, not reindeer."

Coming up on the sunny side of her road was like floating through liquid amber - or dry sherry, she thought, with mischievous recollection of its newly discovered delights. Alcohol at home had meant dark, thick, sweet sherry for their ever rarer guests, a small glass of port each for the threesome to toast Christmas and brandy for medical emergencies. Crossing the road to her door was to plunge into cool dusk and inside the communal lobby she was in total darkness for a moment. She stood at the stair foot groping in bag and pocket for her keys. Then she stopped, head cocked to listen. No sound from the ground floor; the Grants would not be home till seven thirty. The top flat was still vacant. Yet she was sure she had heard something. There was more light from above than could filter through the stained glass fanlight over her front door. She crept up to the angle of the stairs where she could see the top half of that door through the banisters. It was true. Sunlight sliced through where it stood ajar. Suddenly cold, she clutched her jacket round her - there was someone in her flat. Someone was moving about, a shadow crossing and recrossing, intermittently shutting off the sunbeam. Someone was in her flat, moving about among her things. She was being burgled. What was one supposed to do? One should surely not confront the intruder. That would be asking for trouble, would it not? So Nesta would say. A wave of nausea washed over her as she pictured uncaring hands rifling through her things, the gathered shells of her encrusted life, spoiling what they did not understand, like Goths in Rome. All at once she was sick, discreetly into her hat like a lady so as not to contaminate the stairs, and the burglar heard her. For an instant she saw him brilliantly sunlit in the doorway, an unforgettable face, spiky dark brows drawn down against the dazzle, lips stretched back, teeth and eyeballs stained red by the sunset.

She turned and half fell down the stairs. Pausing only a moment the man came pounding after her. She was out of the front door just in time and down the steps right into the arms of a bunch of teenagers milling down the road. Baseball caps and black and purple dragons, Stephen's tormenters, her assailants from Grove Park. She didn't care. It was the burglar's vicious angry face she was frightened of.

"Please, please," she cried, clutching at them as they pressed round her. "Help me, help me, there's a man after me."

"Where? Where?" For he was nowhere to be seen. All the same, laughing and pushing each other, they bore Alice with them along the road, squealing with joy at the irony of it (not that they could have put a name to it) and took her right across town to the police station. They crowded into the reception area, hilariously relishing being on the righteous side of the matter for once. The desk sergeant sorted them out and good-naturedly chased them away, Alice's cries of gratitude ringing in their ears.

She was driven home by a young policewoman. Her front door was standing open but there was no obvious sign of disturbance inside. The policewoman was very polite and kind, settling Alice into an armchair while she made her a cup of tea. She cautioned her to be more careful about closing and properly securing her door and recommended a spyhole so that she could avoid opening it to strangers.

"But I did not let him in," expostulated Alice. "He was there when I arrived home."

"Yes, dear," soothed the policewoman, "but all the same."

Back at the station the story added to the gaiety of nations.

"Poor old bat, nutty as a fruit cake."

"What's she going to come up with next?"

"Got a fixation on that Little gang by the looks."

"Yeah, one minute they're muggers and the next they're her best mates."

"Knights in shining armour no less."

"How about this burglar with the glaring red eyes then?"

"Who doesn't leave any traces." This was the policewoman who had been to the flat.

The sergeant stopped himself in the act of balling Alice's statement. "Better not bin it," he said. "Isn't she a friend of old Ratcliffe's?"

"Who he?" asked the new constable on the desk.

"Used to be something of a big wheel on the Police Authority," the sergeant told him. "Probably still drinks with some of them. He brought her in when she reported that little gang - no pun intended - in the first place."

Slowly recovering her equanimity at home, the poor old bat found that a lot of things had in fact been moved, especially her papers and, for some strange reason, her bed settee, which had not been quite correctly restored to position, but nothing appeared to be missing or even damaged. She couldn't understand it. Her head was thumping; all the pleasures of the day had been driven away. This, she thought, was perhaps a case for testing the therapeutic properties of brandy. She drank a liberal measure of it in hot milk and went to bed early. She felt very strange, as though she had cartwheeled into bed and then it had gone on cartwheeling with her, but she soon went swooping into sleep, dreaming such dreams as made her wish she had stayed awake, cries and groans and a diminuendo of shrieks, over and over and over again.

Chapter Six

Alice struggled out of sleep like a too long submerged swimmer clawing through the interface of water and air. She sat up in a huddle of bedclothes, her head clasped between her two hands, and peered at the window. It was just light, the sunrise pink reflected on the underside of clouds in the west. Desperate for the lavatory she staggered out of bed, meaning to get back into it on her return, but after so dreadful a night she recoiled with some distaste from the idea and went instead to the window, always open to the air when the weather allowed, and took long shuddering breaths of cold air to dispel the rags of her nightmares. Steadying herself against the window sill she leaned forward to savour the dawn, the sky and sea drinking the light, shapes emerging from shadows. There was something on the rocks below, just visible beyond and beneath the parapet of the clifftop walkway. Jetsam from a passing vessel? No, these were neap tides, when the water didn't come up that far. A dark bundle of something was it? As the light grew, colour was beginning to stain the dusky monochromes and outlines were sharpening. It began to look like a person, spread out in starfish fashion seventy feet below her window. A vivid spot of red - a red cap. Stephen had a red cap, the one he used for collecting the money. All her blood seemed to drain into her legs. Her head swam. This was her vision from the time she first saw him. It couldn't be - couldn't - couldn't have been a premonition - could it? No, it wasn't - she was mistaken. He had been cruelly disappointed, day after day, robbed, ravaged even, but surely not - surely he had not been as desperate as that. She ought to have been more sensitive, supportive, reached out to him in his distress, not just signalled the lack of news from her window. Face it, Alice, she upbraided herself, he must have felt you were avoiding him - you were indeed avoiding him - caring more for your own discomfort, your stupid embarrassment, than for his real need. She shook her head convulsively and straightened up. Don't be silly, Alice, she scolded herself, it was probably just some old clothes, she was still in the grip of her dreams. She reached for her birdwatching binoculars to clinch the point. The picture came into focus. There could be no more doubt. It was a body and - her throat tightened - it did look terrifyingly like Stephen. She thought she saw him move.

Now what? Nine nine nine. No good asking for the police; they would never take her seriously after yesterday. She was used to having to circumvent people who did not take her seriously. Daddy never had. Old age had been such a burden for him, poor dear, made him more judgmental than ever.

"Emergency services. Which service do you require?"

"Ambulance please." That was more to the point. He might be alive, please God. Whoever it was down there. Having given her particulars she described what she had seen and explained the topography of the place. "Yes, there are steps all the way down the cliff. No, you cannot get an ambulance as far as that along the promenade because it becomes narrow and there are some steps down and a long flight up. The best way is to stop in the road outside my house and approach by the alley at the side. - Yes, the injured person is right behind my building. - Yes, that is the correct address."

She muddled herself into her clothes and hurried out in time to flag down the ambulance and guide the paramedics through. Then, teeth chattering more from foreboding than the morning chill, she leaned on the wall to watch the men running deftly down the cliff steps with their light stretcher and crouching beside what at this lesser distance she was more and more certain was her boy. They were checking him over, supporting his head with one of those collars. Without being able to distinguish words, she could hear the murmured reassurance of their tones. One of them was now using his radio phone. Her hands were growing numb from their pressure on the wall. At last they had him strapped securely on the frame of the stretcher and began moving carefully over the rocks and easing their burden up the long ladder.

More sirens were arriving, the police of course. The ambulance man must have called them. Alice recognised one of the constables from yesterday, but he didn't notice her. The pair of them went halfway down the cliff to talk to the ambulance men on their way back up. She shifted her cramped hands and found they were sticking to the wall, leaving it with unpleasant reluctance. Puzzled, she studied them and then sniffed. It looked and smelt like half-dried blood on them. She examined the wall, marked with the prints of her hands among the stains. There were spots and splashes on the ground by her feet too. None on her shoes.

The stretcher party had reached the top.

"Thank you, Miss Fairbairn," said the front man as they turned towards the alley. "You can leave him with us now."

Alice trotted by the stretcher, aching for the battered young creature swaddled there in a tight blanket.

"Oh Stephen, Stephen, I am so sorry," she wailed softly.

"That his name? Good. Come along then, Stephen, wake up. You're OK now. We'll soon have you safe in hospital."

The boy opened his eyes and, seeing Alice, gave her a look of such anguished appeal.

"Oh Miss," he whispered, "my poor mum."

And that was all. She watched them get into the ambulance and go, lights and sirens blaring.

The two policemen were strolling up the alley, deep in conversation. Clasping her sticky hands in distress, she was reminded of the blood. Was it - it must be - significant. She pattered after the men.

"Excuse me, officer," she said, spreading her gory hands out. "There is blood on the wall where I was standing, right at the place from which he must have fallen."

The policeman she recognised smiled indulgently at her. "Dear me, Miss Fairbairn" - he winked at his colleague - "you have made a mess of yourself. You want that seeing to. Those stones sure can be sharp, can't they? Take you to Casualty if you like."

Alice shook her head in frustration and slightly overbalanced herself. She was feeling a little giddy. "No officer, thank you, I am not at all hurt. This is not my blood. It is off the wall."

The policemen exchanged grins. "Or she is," muttered the second man.

"If you will bleed all over it, dear! You sure you wouldn't like us to take you into A and E? All that blood, you might be needing a stitch. No? Then you'd better go and have a wash and see what you've done to yourself. Sure you're OK? Know what to do if you find you do need someone? Just ring nine nine nine and there's nothing the ambulance crew would like better than coming to help you, would they Kev?" They exchanged winks again, their chequer-banded caps leaning conspiratorially together.

They went. Stupid creatures, thought Alice. She didn't have much experience of men. Did none of them ever listen, she wondered. These were professionals; they ought to understand the importance of those bloodstains, whatever they were - it was - whatever it was... Whatever what was? Clutching her forehead to steady herself and get the world back into focus, she became aware that something was the matter with her. The brandy? Was this perhaps what was meant by a hangover? Never mind what it was, she had to get herself back indoors. And up the stairs. And in through her front door, which was standing open, as she had left it. What a good thing that policewoman was not there, she told herself, giggling. Then, kicking off her shoes, she fell into bed just as she was. Was her pillow always as hard as this? How could she ever have put up with it? She burrowed her head into it, seeking ease.

The terrible picture of Stephen's smashed-up face forced its way into her mind, his voice - Oh Miss, my poor mum - my poor mum - poor mum - mum - mum - mum - became mingled with the night's cries and shrieks and pounding footfalls as she sank back into her nightmare.

Chapter Seven

Darren Vowles put his head round the ambulance station door, wearing his whipped pooch expression. "Got anything for a poor hungry newshound?" he asked, all eyes and jowls.

The girl on the desk laughed. "Not so's you'd notice it," she said. "Usual moans about being called out for a cut finger or a bad case of the burps. - Oh, Nick and Gary had a nasty one earlier on today, lad on the rocks at Weston. Seems to have chucked himself off the cliff."

"Suicide?" Darren's voice was as lugubrious as the drooping lines of his folded face.

"Attempted - could be. Took him into the Weston General."

"Not much there then." His face twisted into comical wryness. "What's his name?"

"Dunno. They only got as far as Stephen."

"'Mystery Stephen's jump.' - Oh, any idea how old?"

"Nah. Top teens?"

"Might make a filler." Darren made a businesslike note and gave her a cheerful grin, all his facial creases suddenly horizontal. "Cheers." And he was gone.

Peter had embarked on the laborious process of getting out his electric wheelchair. He was beginning to be anxious. Since his return from his family visit two days before, he had tried four times, at carefully judged moments, to get Alice on the phone, wanting to alert her to a snippet in the paper about a 'tragic accident to mystery youth'. He couldn't think who to ask about her; they seemed to have no friends in common. She had mentioned a Nesta and a Daphne, but without their surnames he would get no joy from the telephone book. Stephen might have been able to help, but he had not been at his usual post by Boots's door when Peter trundled along the High Street expressly to find him. Moreover, he had this nasty hunch that Stephen himself might well be the subject of the newspaper reference. What to do? She surely would have mentioned it if she had planned to be away. Or would she? Perhaps he was leaping ahead of himself. Yes, a very independent lady. It was none of his business. Even so he coaxed and bullied his buggy all the way to where she lived. What a place to get at, he reflected, exasperated. For starters it pushed the battery-driven motor to its limits to get up the short steep hill. Then it was four grand but badly worn steps to the house's original entrance, now the door of the ground floor flat, and, worse, a long inelegant concrete flight mounting diagonally across the wall above it that gave access to the converted flats above. Then there would be further stairs above; she lived, he understood, on the second floor. Why would any elderly lady in her right mind purchase a flat situated like that? He immobilised his chair, took his sticks in his hand and pondered. Would the sticks be more hindrance than help? Once he reached the handrail he could probably haul himself up the steps. Just one stick, perhaps? Problems, problems.

"Peter Ratcliffe? Am I right? Am I right? Of course I am."

Peter looked up in surprise at the tall imposing woman in a blue trouser suit and an incongruous pair of rather shabby trainers. One of Alice's U3A friends for sure. What were their names?

"Social Philosophy group?" he ventured.

"Among others. Nesta Harbottle." She extended a strong hand. "Checking up on our mutual friend, eh? Didn't turn up to our opening session this morning. No word. Not like her. Oldfashioned punctilio. So forth. Refreshing that. Endearing too. Bit worried about her consequently. You too?"

Peter nodded. There was neither need nor space for speech.

"Ever been up to her flat? Lovely place. Victoriana intact. Wonderful view. Bit difficult with your sticks. Guess you've never made it. Worry not. Stay put. I'll be back."

With a brisk nod she set off and rang first Alice's bell

and then the two alongside it. Then, impatiently, she pushed at the door and, finding it give, with a tssk of irritation disappeared inside. Peter's anxiety increased as the minutes passed. Nesta came back at last and bent confidentially over his chair, engulfing him with good will and the scent of warm woman.

"Quit fretting. Silly old girl, fit to be tied. Always tell her that."

"Is she ill?"

"Some bug or other. Bit early in the season for flu - haven't even gone for our jabs yet. Been in bed several days, it seems. Never had the wit to ring any of us. Heaven's sake, she's got friends."

"How has she managed, do you know? Meals? Things to drink? How did you get into her flat? Perhaps you have her key...?"

"Have now, no sweat. Came to the door white as a ghost. Dressing gown. No slippers. One gets by, you know. But you can relax. Nesta to the rescue. Madam'll get her nourishment all right now. And clean linen. And a nice bath."

"Has she had a doctor?"

"Bless my stars, no. Wouldn't think of that. Her sort bother God sooner than the doctor. Had enough doctors and pills with the Aged P or Ps. No point now - over the worst. Leave it to me."

And so it was left, Nesta glowing with the importance of a real task, Peter retreating, sadly aware of his inability to do his friend the least service.

The following day Alice did answer his call. "Oh Peter," she said, "I have been so worried."

"But you are on the mend now I hope. At any rate, I'm glad to see you do manage to get to the phone now. Haven't you got an extension by the bed?"

"Yes yes yes - I mean, no I haven't." He made a mental note. "But I am nearly well again, just a trifle unsteady on my pins. Nesta is being so good." She sighed.

"I'm sure she is," he said, smiling grimly to himself. "A most capable lady."

"Yes, indeed." A pause. Then she continued. "Was it you who kept ringing? I am so sorry. I was having such dreadful nightmares and the ringing became part of them. - Oh, I don't mean - that is, it was most kind of you to be concerned about me. But Peter, that is not what I am so worried about. It is Stephen. I rang the hospital just now - I had tried before, several times I think, and never quite seemed to succeed - but this time I did get through, only when I owned up that I was not a relative, they refused to tell me anything." She told him the whole story as best she could, thankful to have an intent concerned listener.

The key sounded in the front door lock.

"That will be Nesta," she interrupted herself, whispering. "I could not possibly - I will ring you later." She could not possibly have confided in poor Nesta was what she meant. Poor Nesta, she was so kind. So kind, at least, in those situations she understood. And what more can any of us do?

Chapter Eight

The Rose had become their favourite rendezvous and so it was thither that Alice's first convalescent steps were bent. Well into October now, the Indian summer was over. She and Peter sat indoors by a wood fire, a scattering of brave blooms on wind-stripped bushes visible through the windows.

"Our equinoctial gales whip round even the sheltered backs of these seafront buildings," observed Peter, watching the Rose's proprietor sweeping up leaves and torn branches.

Alice, gazing intently at him, was not to be distracted. "They allowed you to see him then?" she persisted.

"They did, yesterday morning." He was not going to go on about the difficulties he had faced, firstly the red tape and secondly negotiating the maze of corridors and lifts to the intensive care ward where Stephen, white as a votive candle, had been strung about with wires and tubes. "What he said to you were his last words, my dear. After that he sank into a coma from which he never awoke."

She looked at him, wide-eyed. "You're telling me the boy's dead?"

He covered her supplicating hands with his. "I am very very sorry. This was in this morning's Post. He must have slipped away soon after I saw him." The paper he took from his pocket was folded to reveal the relevant piece. He pushed it over to her, his finger marking the place.

DEATH FALL OF ALLEGED DRUGGIE. The headline screamed at her. 'An unidentified youth of no fixed abode has died in the Weston General Hospital. He was found with multiple injuries at Anchor Head, a favourite beauty point, fifteen days ago. He never regained consciousness. It is thought he had thrown himself over the cliff under the influence of drugs. The death is not regarded as suspicious. The police are trying to trace any family.'

Alice sat suddenly very erect, eyes wide and angry, cheeks patched with red in a white face. "How dare they?" she cried. "How dare they? 'Druggie' indeed. Stephen was not a drug addict. Oh poor child - dead - how can they insult the dead like that? 'The death is not regarded as suspicious'! As though it can be written off as of no importance! Unfortunate he was, very very unhappy, but whatever had gone wrong in his life it was not drugs. I am absolutely certain of that."

"Gently, Alice. You're not really fit yet. Calm down."

"Calm down! Calm down! How can I calm down? These terrible lies are blackening the boy. Doesn't he have enough to contend with without that? He has been trying so hard - and everything against him. What was he expecting from those exam results, Peter? What he was saying to us so recently was a million miles away from drug addiction and despair. Oh - it makes me so furious!"

"So I see, my dear," said Peter, capturing the hand she was beating the table with. "It makes me angry too, but we mustn't break the china."

"No," she agreed, immediately contrite. "But if we don't defend him, who will? He is at the bottom of the pile; anyone can kick him. And they do. It is too much for him to bear alone."

"But Alice, my dear old girl, we don't actually know what it was he had to bear, do we, or why he was here and homeless at all. We found him a very appealing and seemingly genuine young man, but we do know extraordinarily little about him."

She looked at him in amazement. "Yes, I suppose that is true. But I do know this; he is not a drug addict."

"*Was* not a drug addict."

Alice looked wildly round. Snatching back her hands, she clutched at her head for a moment. Then, steadying herself, resting her palms on the table, she spoke quietly. " "*Was* not a drug addict. Nor was he a suicide. He was murdered, Peter."

There was a long pause. They could hear each other

breathing and the fire flickering, snap, snap.

"What makes you say that?"

"The blood on the wall, Peter. There was a lot of blood on the wall and the pavement exactly where he must have gone over - been pushed over. He had been seriously injured before his fall, Peter."

They went together to the police station where, in honour of Peter's past membership of the Police Authority, they were ushered into the relative comfort of the inner sanctum and a young policeman brought them coffee, instant, but in real china cups with Hobnobs in the saucers. A senior detective listened courteously as Peter outlined the story in a few succinct words. Finding nothing in the case notes to indicate Alice's involvement in the incident, the officer was puzzled at first.

"It was I who summoned the ambulance," she insisted. "Not your good selves, because I had seen movement and felt that medical help was the more urgent need."

"Quite right, Miss Fairbairn, you did very well." The officer regarded her kindly. He had heard all the stories, the muggers who turned into heroes, the phantom burglar, everything. In the presence of ex-councillor Ratcliffe this had to be played with extreme care. "I understand that you had befriended this unfortunate lad, Miss Fairbairn. Very commendable, I must say, if a tad risky. It's sometimes better, and safer, to leave these cases to the professionals. That's my advice to you."

"Which advice might indeed be sound if the professionals were actually becoming involved or even showing the slightest interest," retorted Alice tartly, "but they were not. Instead the poor boy was left entirely to his own resources up until the tragedy and publicly insulted after it. Just because he was destitute, have the papers the right to blazon him a drug addict and a suicide? I know he was neither of these things. How dare anyone write somebody off like that?"

"I quite agree," soothed the inspector. "This reporter has overstepped the mark. It was probably a tragic misadventure. But put your mind at ease, madam. The autopsy will show whether or not drugs were involved, though the length of time between the injuries and death will complicate matters. At least the hospital found no evidence of alcohol."

Alice found herself trembling again. She slopped her coffee into her saucer, where her Hobnob took care of it, collapsing into soggy inedibility. "I know he did not take drugs," she persisted. The detective cocked an eye at her, head on one side like a bird on sentry go. She plunged on: "And I also know he did not commit suicide."

"And what brings you to that conclusion?"

"He was expecting his A level results."

The inspector regarded her gravely, controlling the twitch at the corner of his mouth. "I see."

"He had so much to look forward to, you understand." Alice's eyes were scalded with tears now.

"Indeed." A sympathetic smile.

Peter felt it was time he took a hand. "Miss Fairbairn is convinced she has positive evidence that this young man, Stephen, was murdered."

"Stephen? You know his name sir? We've been trying to trace his next of kin."

"Not his surname, I'm afraid."

"Any other details that might help us sir?"

"Stoke-on-Trent," said Peter, suddenly. "I saw it on an envelope he was addressing to his mother. I'm sure of it."

"He only left school in July," added Alice.

"Many thanks indeed," said the detective, rising and politely indicating that the interview was over. "You've been extremely helpful. Sir. Madam."

"But my evidence," objected Alice. "You've forgotten the blood."

The officer paused a moment. "Blood, Miss Fairbairn?"

"The blood on the wall. Mr. Ratcliffe did mention it to you. And I pointed it out to the policeman at the time."

"The officer who attended the scene of the incident? I'll certainly look into it, Miss Fairbairn."

"Thank you, officer. I should be so glad if you would. I expect all the blood on the wall will have been washed way by the rain by this time, but you may have my coat in evidence. I fear I have not brought it with me on this occasion, but rest assured, I

45

have not had time to have it cleaned; I have been ill, you know. In any case I had surmised that it might be needed for forensic investigation."

"That would be most helpful, Miss Fairbairn. May I relieve you of your coffee cup?" Firmly, with politeness that bordered on gallantry, the inspector saw them out.

"By the by," he asked no-one in particular on his way back through the main office, "who was it went to the cliff top incident ten days ago?"

A young constable searching for some data on his computer looked up brightly. "I did, sir. Me and Kevin Bradley."

"What's this Miss Fairbairn's saying about blood? I don't remember any mention of blood in your report."

The young man bent his head, nether lip jutting. Stupid old bag, he thought, and shook himself smartly erect again. "The lady had hurt her hand on the wall where she was leaning to watch us, sir. She was bleeding all over the place. We would have taken her to A and E sir, but she wouldn't go. We did offer, sir. Especially as she seemed, well, a bit confused, sir."

There was a smothered snort of laughter from Kevin on the other side of the room.

"Well?" barked the inspector. "You got something to add, Bradley?"

Kevin straightened up. The old man must be in a mood about something. "No sir, but we know the lady of old, sir, a nice old lady and all that but, well, shall we say a bit romantic, sir?"

So that was all there was to it, mused the inspector, finishing his own cold coffee as he stood gazing out of the window. He had thought old Ratcliffe's head was better screwed on than that, but that's friendship for you - he was probably fond of the old duck. It was a bit of a relief anyway. The last thing they wanted just now was a murder investigation, especially into the death of a piece of flotsam like this lad. Homeless kids - where did they all come from? There hadn't been any about when he was a lad himself; you never saw a beggar or a street sleeper then. Broken homes and so on, yes, but hadn't there always been unsatisfactory families? Some folks thought drop-outs were scum, hardly human. The Miss Fairbairns, at the other extreme, went all dewy-eyed over them -

just as wrong-headed as the bring-back-the-birch-brigade. Maybe Gilford of the Sally Army came closest to a sane approach. But meanwhile, if the kid had got himself into that kind of mess, no wonder if he jumped, poor sod.

Chapter Nine

Peter saw Alice home by taxi. He would have given a lot to be able to escort her safely up all those stairs to her flat and settle her down with a cup of coffee, with maybe something a little stronger in it. She was so white and over controlled, as though the flick of a fingernail would set her ringing like fine porcelain or shatter her like crystal at a crucially pitched note. But bone china was amazingly tough, he reminded himself, and the odds against crystal being struck by the exact and only sound that would shatter it were enormous. She seemed to have survived the first shock by turning grief into anger, a healthy reaction. In any case, he told himself mournfully, those stairs might as well be Everest as far as he was concerned. He watched from the taxi until he saw her wave from the landing window, then told the driver to take him home, Poor Stephen, he reflected, with what longing, with what mounting sense of dread he must have stood watching that landing window for a signal that his letter had come. Peter made a mental note that he must not bring her to that window again.

Alice turned abruptly from her lookout point in an effort to shut out the image of the young face in which she had seen day by day the brutal destruction of hope. The westering sun was filling her sitting room with an autumnal smudge of golden light. These were the windows through which she had seen his body spread-eagled derelict on the rocks. It was down there on the path she had heard his last words, 'Oh Miss, my poor Mum...' On an impulse she drew the heavy curtains across and stood in artificial dusk. Wherever she looked there were windows, windows with tragedy behind them. She closed all the other curtains too and shrouded the flat in gloom. Poor child - did nobody love him? Nobody but her, that is, and that was hardly to the purpose. Did the mother to whom his thoughts turned when he was dying - not wailing for her comfort as grown men, even soldiers in battle did, according to the books, but concerned for her - did she not love him? Why had he left home in the first place? He was only a child. Images followed each other across her mind's eye: Stephen embarrassed; Stephen soaking wet and forlorn; alight with the pleasures of poetry; humiliated; angry; arrogant; drunk with vistas of the future, full of eager anticipation - a wisp of hair coiled in the tender hollow of his nape, so heart-stoppingly young, stretched for the axe - hope draining away from him drop by drop - Stephen broken on the rocks. 'Oh Miss, my poor mum...'

Alice sat down heavily on the settee, bowed her head to her knees and began to sob, painfully at first, hard and dry, and then the tears began to flow. She mourned for this young stranger as she had never done for her parents. She had loved them dearly, of course, but they were so old, had for so long been more like her children than her parents, but children in reverse, with no future to look forward to. Daddy would have been a hundred and twenty now if he could have lived, one of Swift's struldrugs. After Mummy too had died she had woken up to find that she was old herself. Where had her life gone? She was grieving for the waste of Stephen's young life, the squandering of his golden promise, but also for the loss of her own past. Any future she had still to look forward to was likely to be even shorter than the life Stephen had had to look back on, his childhood, her senescence. She wept tears of long-pent, deeply suppressed bitterness until it was all flushed away, leaving her with a new-washed sense of the unfairness of the present. She sat up and wiped her face. If her future was to be short, all the more reason to make good use of it. The first thing she must do, she determined, was to take her coat to the police station and make them analyse those bloodstains. Then she must find Stephen's mum. Meeting him had brought her face to face with the injustices of life and where injustice was, if she could she must fight it.

She took her stained coat to the police station the first thing next morning. The desk sergeant had been primed for her arrival, polite but formal. He put the coat in a plastic cover, labelled it and gave her a receipt. He asked her if she would oblige by allowing the police surgeon to take a sample of her own blood, 'for purposes of comparison.'

Alice was astonished. "Whatever relevance can my blood possibly have?" she demanded.

"Probably absolutely none, madam." Though in the light of station gossip, that was not his real view at all. "For purposes of elimination. Just routine procedure, you understand."

"No, I do not understand," she said, but submitted meekly to the drawing off of the required thimbleful. The glowing resolve that had followed her fit of grief the day before was being smothered by this dispassionate behemoth of bureaucracy. Walking briskly to fight off the onset of despondency, she decided to go home by the sea front. To gaze across the bay, burnished pewter today under a pearly sky as she made her way along the almost deserted out-of-season promenade, would calm and lift her spirits. At its northern end the parade swept grandly westward, ran skittishly down broad steps to the sandy Madeira Cove and up again, round the long disused band stand, up again by some fifty narrower curving steps and sobered into the mere walkway that skirted Anchor head, running between that fateful cliff and the back of Alice's towering flats. As she climbed she began to panic at her folly in having come that way, the first time since the tragedy. Suddenly a rush of feet heralded the arrival of a gang of boys round the bend above her. She flattened herself against the offshore wall as they came blundering by like a herd of young bullocks out to grass.

Their leader jerked to a stop in front of her. "Hi Miss. Sorry. Didn't mean to bash you." He wore the black and purple T shirt she remembered from their previous encounters; apparently these young creatures did not feel the autumn chill. The other lads returned, inquisitive, grinning and pushing each other with little snorts of laughter.

Alice looked at them, controlling her breathing, the high wall at her back. They were only children, she reminded herself, ignorant thoughtless children, full of untutored energy, bouncing and battering the world to find out where they stood in it. As she had been herself once, within so much tighter confines, but longing for understanding and forgiveness of her mistakes. They 'didn't mean to bash her' - of course they did not. She winced at the memory of the terrifying hours she had spent locked in the cupboard under the stairs 'thinking over her naughtiness' - 'Daddy, I didn't mean to do it - I didn't mean to.' Poor Father, she supposed he had meant it all for her own good, but how she had longed to be believed. She made up her mind.

"Hallo, all of you," said Alice. "You have not hurt me at all, I am glad to say. How are you getting on? No school today?"

"Half term, Miss. One of our best places, along there." He flicked a thumb over his shoulder. "We dig bait for our dads along under the toll road. Tide's out, innit."

"You're fishermen, then?"

"When we get the chance. Fishing was real big round here in Grandad's day. Fed all Bristol he said. Dad just picks up enough for us dinner, if the tide's right of a weekend."

"That is nice." Alice smiled less tightly, warming to them. She remembered how angry and helpless she had felt at these boys for their bullying of Stephen, their callous destruction of his precious things, how they had jostled and robbed herself, alien, hostile entities. But now she could clearly see them as overgrown little boys, their lives as dangerously free as hers had been cloistered. She was glad she had refused to press charges against them; they would hardly have been so friendly now if she had. There were better ways for them to learn where the boundaries were, what was acceptable behaviour and what was not. What she could not understand or forgive was their treatment of Stephen. Why had they done it?

"I am Miss Fairbairn," she ventured. "Now tell me your name, turn and turn about you know."

"Rob. Rob Little."

Alice made a wry grimace. "Well, I admit you did not rob me of much."

Miss!" Rob's tone was hurt and indignant. "You! That's not... Anyway, my dad says you were all right about that. 'Let that be a lesson to you', he says."

"I am very glad. How old are you, Rob?"

"Fifteen next month."

"Fifteen." Alice sighed. "You will soon be a man."

"Yup." The boy squared his shoulders, conscious of their

budding muscles. "Not seen that burglar again, then?"

"Fortunately no. Thank you for helping me that day."

"No big deal." His beaming smile and puffed chest belied his words.

On a snatched breath she got it out: "Why did you destroy the homeless boy's property?"

There was a stirring among the group. Rob was taken aback, but not embarrassed. "Well Miss, we was just having a bit of fun. He's just a piece of shit" - Alice determined to find out what the word meant, having by now heard it used several times in a derogatory sense - "and he treated us like he was better than us."

"You know he is dead."

Now she had all their attention. They were visibly shocked.

"No, Miss, man. How can he be? Mum says them sort always do all right, sponging off of the rest of us lot. He wasn't starving or nothing was he? We never meant him no harm. What he die of then?"

"I believe someone killed him."

They were wide-eyed and silent for a long moment.

"What'd anyone want to do that for then? Poor little sod."

One of the others spoke. "It wasn't him went over the cliff back of your place then Miss, was it?"

"Yes. But he was not a drug addict."

"Must 'a' been. It was in the paper." Their faces cleared, the matter having been settled to their satisfaction. They gave her a thumbs up and were off in a swirl like starlings.

Alice sighed and, resisting the temptation to look over into the cove or pay attention to the wall, went by way of the side alley round to the front door and back home. She rang Peter and gave him an account of her morning's adventures.

"If you haven't got round to lunch yet," he said, "Stay put till you hear my car horn and we'll go out for it. Somewhere nice, a stately home or the cathedral at Wells. Or even a village pub. It would do us both good to get away for a few hours. You be thinking where you would like to go while you're waiting."

Later, after a pleasant, rather late lunch in the cloister

restaurant, they sat over their coffee, looking out over the square with its few modest black crosses marking the discreet resting places of the more recently departed dignitaries. Alice sighed a long shuddering sigh.

"Peter," she said, "they do not take me seriously, the police. They just humour me because they think I am a poor dotty old thing who is going wrong in the head. As far as they are concerned Stephen can be written off as one of life's failures, sad, but not worth a second thought. They resist the bother of pursuing proper enquiries. Did I tell you? They actually asked the police doctor to take a sample of my own blood, mine! Whatever could they want that for? 'For purposes of comparison' they said. Now whyever would they do that, except to pull the wool over my eyes?"

"They do need to prove the bloodstains on the coat are not yours, you know."

"Ah. Yes. I see. But, Peter, we must find Stephen's mother. We can do it. There cannot be so many secondary schools in Stoke-on-Trent that we cannot track down the one from which a seventeen year old boy named Stephen left last summer having just taken A levels in English, Psychology and Spanish -"

"Not to mention Latin at GCSE. You're perfectly right, Alice. Good for you. I'll check out the Education Year Book in the Library tomorrow and write to the head teachers."

They went into the cathedral nave to listen to the choir practising Thomas Tallis, absorbing the tranquil lights and shadows of the soaring stones and lambent glass. Then, much refreshed, they took a slow route home in the long late-afternoon light, through lanes gaudy with tattered foliage and bright scarlet splashes of hips and haws in the blowsy hedges.

Chapter Ten

Peter trundled along to the public library the next morning, where the abstracted young woman at the enquiry desk fetched the Education Year Book down from the reference section for him. There were quite a number of secondary schools in Stoke, of which the sixth form college was the obvious one to try. He noted all their addresses and the names of the head teachers just in case, returned the volume with thanks and made his way back home to his word processor. Really he ought to invest in a computer, he thought, and go on the net. The rest of his day was spent framing polite letters to the schools, enquiring for the address of one Stephen, surname unknown, possibly an ex-pupil of theirs, who had taken four A levels in his subjects the previous summer, not forgetting the distinctive Latin GCSE. Catching the last collection from the box on the corner, he sighed the sigh of a job well done and rang Alice to tell her all about it.

"Oh Peter, bless you," she said. "I've been thinking maybe Captain Gilford might be another line to try. He did say at that meeting that he knew all the homeless people in town."

"Stephen didn't have much use for that gentleman, if you remember. And the police have probably tried him already. Still, can't do any harm. I'll give him a ring. Tomorrow morning suit you, if he's free then?"

The captain elected to come to Peter's house. On this her first visit there, Alice restrained her curiosity, limiting herself to what she needed to see to navigate her way through the hall to a bright room, where she accepted a chair with a view through long windows at a sunny garden ringed with fruit trees. Peter in his home environment was a new experience which, given time, if so it was to be, would round out and enrich her perception of him. Wary and uncertain of her position meanwhile, she saw as it were through tunnel vision, focussing clearly only on the faces of the two men. Peter was talking easily to the captain. His words began to emerge into her consciousness.

"... not taken into his confidence I gather."

"No, you have to respect that," conceded the captain. "A very bruised young man I fear. Not ready or willing to accept help. I kept as close an eye on him as I could, all the same. The prouder and more independent these folk are, the more they are at risk, as, of course, events were sadly to demonstrate. I said as much to Cornford. Tragic, tragic."

"You've had speech with Inspector Cornford then?"

"Naturally. Anything to do with the local social misfits, first thing the police do is call on me."

"Ah," said Peter, with an amused glance at Alice, "beat us to it on that one, as we guessed, my dear."

"I'm afraid I couldn't help much since, sad to say, I had not succeeded in penetrating the boy's defences -"

And I think you would never have done so, thought Alice rebelliously.

"- though the onset of the really cold weather might have broken through them. But he had been going downhill fast, I felt, and for some reason he had shifted his base."

"Those boys who wear the dragon T shirts, Rob Little and his friends you know, they drove him out from under the railway arch," put in Alice suddenly.

Captain Gilford regarded her with new respect. She coloured.

"Oh no," she protested. "I was not so privileged. It was quite by chance that I saw what happened. Poor boy, he never knew there had been a witness, thank goodness. He would have died of shame."

There was an appalled hush as they all realised what she had said.

"See that blackbird," the captain observed at length, massaging his chin as he gazed out of the window. "Poor wretched thing, it's positively skulking along under that lavender hedge."

"It's the magpies," rejoined Peter, wearily. "They took every one of his fledglings last Spring, two broods. And now they won't leave him alone."

"A cruel world," said the captain, busy with his chin for another silent moment. He straightened up. "None of us seems to have got very far with this unfortunate young man, I'm afraid, though Miss Fairbairn seems to have come closer than most. Never even got his name did we."

"He had such plans," she said, and choked on it. Peter laid a gentle hand on her shoulder.

"You're convinced he did away with himself, aren't you," he said to the captain. It was not a question. "And told Cornford as much."

"Indeed I did. I gave him my honest opinion when asked. But" - he went on - "maybe I should have had another little chat with him."

"Do you know how long it takes the scientific people, the investigators, to report their findings back to the police?" asked Alice.

"How do you mean?" The captain was startled.

"Cause of death? Toxicology? Matching blood samples, that sort of thing?" Peter was trying to clarify matters.

"Oh, cause of death would probably be established immediately at the autopsy. Anything else, drugs, blood, that would go to forensics I presume."

"Yes?"

"It's been privatised you know, forensics. Everything has to be sent away and paid for out of funds."

"How long then?"

"Weeks. Months even, I believe."

Alice was outraged. "Even when it's urgent? Murder cases, for instance?"

"I've never been involved in a murder case myself, only unexplained deaths where there's no reason to suspect foul play, as here."

Peter put out a calming hand to Alice. "But supposing it were, would there be a fast track procedure?" he persisted.

"There must be. It's probably a question of cost."

"But, Captain Gilford," burst out Alice, "how can you say that there is no reason to suspect foul play here? And..." She began to shake. "What does cost..."

"How about making us all a cup of coffee, my dear," said Peter. "Come and see how well organised I am in my kitchen. The captain will excuse us for a few moments."

But the captain excused himself instead and thoughtfully took his leave.

"The audience did seem extremely enthusiastic," said Alice uncertainly. Nesta had thought she needed a change and that a visit to the afternoon performance of the U3A Autumn Revue would be just the thing.

Daphne had joined them. "Naturally. People love seeing their friends make idiots of themselves," she said.

"Elsie was good, wasn't she."

"My dear Alice, girl's capable of so much more than that. Ought to set her sights on proper drama."

"Oh, come off it, Nesta," said Daphne. "You're an old stuffed shirt! What's wrong with a bit of how's your father? And she's still got a dam' good pair of pins on her for a gal of nearly seventy - why shouldn't she show 'em off?"

"Does she have to show quite so much of them though?" wondered Alice. "It made me feel distinctly uneasy, especially with that gentleman looking right up at her from the front row. I hate to think what he could..."

"What gentleman? What was the matter with him?" demanded Daphne.

"The tall one with the bald head who keeps putting his arm round us and doing a kind of gurgle in his throat."

"Oh, him. He's rather an old darling is Derek. Just lonely, poor old stick. You did know he lost his wife in the Spring, didn't you?"

"No, I did not," said Alice. What was that supposed to mean? People should keep their grief to themselves, not embarrass everyone round them. That is what she had always tried to do, as her parents had taught her. Then with a pang of conscience she remembered how kind and supportive these same two friends had been to her when she had arrived, bereaved and alone, a perfect stranger in their midst after her mother's death and how much she owed them. And, faced with her present troubles, how much she owed to Peter.

Nesta's dominant contralto had re-entered the conversation, "...question of standards, whatever you do. 'Man's reach should exceed his grasp' and all that."

Daphne shrieked with glee. "All the way up the fishnets?"

"Fishnets?"

"Oh Alice, you really are! Elsie's come-hither stockings. They come out every year."

"Oh." Alice blushed. Daphne's want of delicacy so often caught her off her guard.

"Saw Elsie play in 'Waiting In The Wings' last year, the dotty one who sets fire to the place. Lovely bit of work. Touched the old heart."

"I know, Nesta," agreed Daphne. "I cried buckets. But she knew what she was talking about; looked after her mother at home as long as she could. That was Alzheimers."

"Tragic way for anyone to go, especially someone gifted. Didn't see that, Alice old girl, did you? Before you arrived on the scene, what. - Alice? Alice? You all right?"

"We oughtn't to have brought her - she's not really fit yet..."

Alice's eyes were brimming. "I'm perfectly well, thank you, truly." But the words came with a sob. "It's just that, well, you see, you were saying what a tragic way for a gifted..."

"Not still fretting over that stalker of yours? Buck up, old thing. Seen the paper? Turns out we were right about the drugs. Don't waste heart on a loser."

"But you are wrong about him, Nesta."

"Oh, come on, my love! Everyone knows he was a druggie. I know it's sad, sweetie pie, but honestly, they have only themselves to blame. Best forget him, darling, and concentrate on getting better."

"Shut up, Daphne." Nesta was regarding Alice, whose tears were oozing down her pinched white face from between her clenched eyelids. "Get a taxi chop chop. Got to get this lady back to bed."

Alice had to contain herself for over a week before the answers from the head teachers began to come in and then they were a disappointment, polite but uninformative. Pussyfooting blighters, thought Peter, exasperatedly, too busy looking over their shoulders to see what was in front of them. Data Protection my eye. He said as much to Inspector Cornford when they chanced to meet in The London Inn and had a quiet pint together. "Can't blame them though, can you," mused the inspector. "We've all got somebody looking over our shoulders nowadays. In any case you can rest easy. We've traced the family and got identification, thanks to you and Miss Fairbairn. We'd've got them sooner or later from dental records, of course, but it only took half an hour for the chaps in Stoke to come up with the goods from the schools. They don't play hard to get with us. Matter of fact, could have been the police query reminded them to be cagey in their letters to you."

Peter regarded him gravely, aware of the irony of the policeman's own reticence. "So you got identification?" he ventured.

"We did sir. The stepfather came down."

"Not the mother?"

"No. Apparently she was away on a touring holiday with girl friends. She was in dire need of a break, he said. The lad had given them a lot of grief, taking off like that as soon as he left school. They had had no idea where he could have gone." The inspector's cheerful open face was giving nothing away.

"No thoughts on why he had done that?"

"You know what kids are like these days. Well, I suppose seventeen and eighteen year olds have kicked over the traces all down the ages; we only think they're worse now because they're in our faces. - Anyway, the chap was anxious to spare her further distress, wanted to break it to her himself as soon as she got back. Fair enough."

So he wasn't going to be drawn. Peter changed tack. "Any further with how it happened? You must have the medical evidence by now."

A momentary flicker of the eyes betrayed the officer's unease. "Of course. You'll have seen the newspaper report. Cause of death was skull fracture with massive brain trauma, though any of the extensive injuries, coupled with exposure, would have been enough. All consistent with the fall, but -". He hesitated. "We might be taking another look at that."

"Ah," said Peter. "Been talking to Gilford?"

The inspector cocked a wary eyebrow.

"And what about the blood on Alice's coat? I understand it's possible, at a price, to fast-track forensics."

The inspector threw back his head and gave a bark of laughter. "I see we've both been talking to him," he said.

Chapter Eleven

"Come on, old girl, shake a leg! Stir your stumps!" said Nesta to Alice encouragingly. She was still popping round to check on her, aware that she was not yet her usual self and conscience-stricken about the expedition to the Autumn Revue. "Take it out of you, these nasty bugs. Can't let them beat you. Let it go at our age and you never get it back."

"Use it or lose it," quoted Alice distractedly

"Bang on," agreed Nesta with enthusiasm. "Good girl. What's to do now then? Walkies?" She looked out across the fog-blacked bay. "Maybe no. Shopping to do? No? Tomorrow's another day. Ride out somewhere in the pesky Peugeot?"

"All the places to visit are shut for the winter, "Alice said.

"Well, 'be prepared' and all that – et voila!" Nesta opened her shopping bag and triumphantly produced a packet of crumpets. "Don't move," she ordered. "Should know my way around by now."

"'I have a toasting fork," Alice ventured. "There is no need to bother with the grill."

They sat by the fire and toasted crumpets and ate a companionable tea. "wicked, this melting butter," gloated Nesta, licking her fingers. "Runs all over you. Gorgeous though, eh? Do a fly weight like you nowt but good. Could do with some feeding up. Seriously, my girl, taken a pasting. Need bucking up, tonic or something. Holiday somewhere warm?"

"I have never been abroad," confessed Alice. What she could not confess in this company was that, though it was true that she still felt washed-out, her lassitude was mostly heartache.

"Had a visit from the boys in blue then?" asked Nesta suddenly.

Alice was taken aback. "Why do you ask?"

"You will, mark my words. Great excitement down my road. Doing house to house. Routine enquires, so-called. 'Where were you on the night of September the twentieth', all that stuff'" She stopped for a moment, looking at Alice. "Day we went out with old Daph, that. Not that blasted revue, no, the Killerton trip. Told the bobby. Not interested, natch. But right under your window, must've heard something, anyone'd think. Sure to come to you. Nearest to the scene of the crime."

"Scene of the crime?" repeated Alice cautiously. It sounded if the inspector had come round to her view after all. True, Peter had thought that Gilford might do the trick.

"That stalker of yours, poor devil. Turns out it was foul play."

Alice's voice was faint. "That was the night I started to be ill, you remember."

"Was it? Had such a good day an' all. Insisted on walking up alone. Remember that."

And came home to so shocking an experience. Why had she never told Nesta anything about it? Never mind; the moment had passed. Strange how those young ruffians had been such a comfort then, Rob Little and his friends.

What sort of telepathic intuition was it that touched off Nesta's next remark? "Told 'em about those juvenile delinquents who knocked you down in the park. Ought to have seen 'em charged. Soft as butter, you. Told you at the time."

"The purple dragon boys? What about them?"

"Yours truly wasn't the first to bring 'em up. Tales came out from all sides. Always up and down the headland, pushing and shoving. Egging each other on. Language to blister you. Your stalker a regular target of theirs, folk say. Eleanor Jones saw them hassling him that very morning. Things they called him – no, don't want to offend your virgin ears duckie. Pushed him right off the pavement she said. One small step from pushing him off the cliff."

Alice was appalled. "Surely not, Nesta! Those boys are only children."

"James Bulger, remember?"

"But Nesta, they had gone by then. They were actually leaving the area that evening just at the time when I arrived home. I – I ran into them."

"My dear old bird, doesn't mean a thing. Up and down all hours all over town. Back and forth. Especially along this end of the front."

"How do you know?" but she knew it was true. If the tide was right they would be digging bait for their fathers, they had told her.

"Everyone's seen them. All hours. Don't know what their parents are thinking of. Dam' good idea you know, child curfew, Labour inspired or not."

Alice was silent, her eyes on the fog-white window. 'Let that be a lesson to you, my dad says', she remembered. That did not sound like a bad parent to her. People had such differing ways of dealing with matters, did they not? And growing boys need more space to explore than they were probably able to have at home.

Nesta eyed her affectionately. Her voice softened. "Poor old Alice. Look thoroughly done in. Better get a bit of shut eye after lunch. Can I get a bit of something for you? No?" Her gaze shifted bleakly to the blank window. "All right. I know. I'll leave you to it. Too much of a good thing, me. Sometimes." She achieved a grin.

"Oh Nesta," cried Alice, coming alive to her "what a very good thing you are!"

Later Peter rang and she told him all about it. "And Peter," she added, "this morning I was doing the dusting – pray, no teasing, I do do it sometimes, though not to the standards mother used to expect – and I saw some men down by the wall. They had delineated it with blue tape, quite an area, and they were scraping away at the stones. One of them squatted down and was scrabbling at the tarmac. Silly things, I said to myself, looking for blood I expect. It will all have been washed away by this time, the weather we have been having. Talk about closing the stable door."

"They may still get something," he assured her. "At any rate you can't say that they aren't taking it seriously any more.

They've got an incident room set up – under Cornford; he's in overall charge of the investigation – and they've got a dozen officers in from other districts to help."

Fog or no fog, she was obliged to do a little shopping the following morning. The post office was of that endangered species which is combined with a brisk little general store. The shop being particularly crowded, she stood waiting her turn, basket in hand. Everyone there was agog with news.

"About time too, little varmints," she heard someone say. It dawned on her that they were talking about Rob Little and the dragon boys and she lowered her well-drilled embargo on personal eavesdropping. Clearly the house-to-house enquiries had stirred longstanding resentments about their loutish behaviour into a storm of general condemnation. Stephen had been correspondingly metamorphosed from no-good scrounger to martyr overnight. Alice listened with growing horror to the vicious flights of fancy, attributing ever blacker deeds to the villains of the hour.

"It was them knocked down that sweet little old lady in Grove Park, you remember."

- "Stole all her jewellery" -

- "She's only just out of hospital, you know" -

- "Poor little soul – I know her well, a more innocent you never..." -

- "Don't know why they weren't put away for that" -

Alice realised with a shock that they were talking about her. What a lying jade Dame Rumour is.

- "Law's too soft – kids these days think they can thumb their noses at anyone" -

- "Bobbies have got their hands tied behind their backs."

Shuffling along in line, Alice had reached the newspaper stand by the counter. A headline in the local paper screamed at her: CLIFF DEATH TEENAGER QUEERBASHERS HELD. Aghast, she reached for the paper just as the hubbub died away, a single voice clear at the end, "I blame the pare...', cut off in embarrassment. A dumpy little woman had come into the shop; face flushed and swollen, hair awry. Silently the crowd squeezed aside, leaving her free to collect her bread, milk and tea and take it unimpeded straight to the checkout. The din broke out more excitedly than ever as the door closed behind her.

"She's got a nerve!"

Alice dumped her basket of as yet unbought goods and hurried out of the shop. Head down, the dumpy woman was crouched by the pillar box. Her plastic grocery bag had split and she was trying to bundle its contents up in its blowing remnants.

"Here," said Alice, "I have a spare bag in my pocket."

The woman looked up in numb gratitude. Alice held the mouth of the bag open for her to put her things in.

"Are you by any chance Mrs. Little?"

"What of it?" retorted the woman, avoiding her eye.

"I know your boy, Rob. He is a rascal – has sometimes done some dreadful things – but I truly believe he never intends real harm. Can you tell me what has happened?"

Mrs. Little squinted up at her through swollen eyelids, suddenly voluble between sobbing breaths. "He's down the nick. Since yesterday. And his mates too. Separate. His dad's there to see fair play if he can. They're only lads, kid's stuff and that. The Bill came and took their clothes away in see-through bags. Had the trainers off of their feet. His old ones I was saving for young Roly as well. I wouldn't care, only he's got nothing left to walk in. He never done nothing, my Rob, never."

Alice thought about that. "At any rate, whatever else he may have done, I am quite sure he did not commit murder."

Mrs. Little crumpled into tears. "Thank you, oh thank you, Miss –"

"Fairbairn."

"You that Miss Fairbairn my Rob...?"

"Yes, indeed I am. That is now all water under the bridge. I believe he has learned his lesson, as he told me his wise father advised him."

"Oh miss, he has."

"And I am absolutely certain he is innocent of murder."

Mrs. Little was past speech. Head down, she set off down the alley. Alice went back for her shopping.

Nesta came up with her at the bottom of her hill. "Here, give me that!" she took the shopping basket. "Silly girl, you know I'd get it for you, independent madam you are. What's got your tongue? Overdoing it? Just whacked? Or worried about something"

Alice smiled a trifle wanly. "Would you explain something for me please, Nesta? I am sure you can enlighten me; what are 'queerbashers'?"

Nesta's full throated laugh was famous in her circles. "Oh my dear Alice," she said when she had done, "you really don't want to know. Here, hold this a mo while I wipe my eyes."

"But I do want to know," objected Alice. "It was a headline in the Post: 'teenage queerbashers held'."

"Particularly unpleasant form of persecution. Like blackbirds picking on one with a lot of white feathers."

What is it about blackbirds and persecution, wondered Alice. Aloud she asked, "You mean singling out for unkind treatment someone who is strange in some way, a hunchback for instance?"

"Dear me, Alice, 'nother thing not to say. Not politically correct, 'hunchback'. Has to be 'physically challenged', some such rot."

"But that apart, and I confess I do find these strictures extremely confusing, am I correct?"

"Nearly. 'Bashing' is real violence. Beating, kicking, so on. And 'queer'? Try 'gay'? 'pansy'? 'nancyboy'? That more your vintage? No? I give up. Try your OED for 'homosexual'."

Alice had to be content. She would ask Peter. She had a lurking feeling it has something to do with Oscar Wilde. And that nice John Betjeman's little friend Teddy; she had never felt she understood that poem, in the light of other people's reaction to it.

'Once there was a man called Oscar Wilde'. Yes? And? Ah well.

She nodded off after lunch, to be startled into wakefulness by the entry phone. The disembodied voice sounded hoarse and wretched.

"Miss, do you mind? I've brought my dad."

Mr. Little was a surprise. Rob, big as he seemed among his friends, had a lot of growing to do in the next four or five years if he was to match him. The boy appeared distinctly small in this context, the more so as the oversized shoes on his feet were obviously not his own. His face looked pinched and recently scrubbed, red around the eyes. His father's was grey, deeply graven with fatigue and worry. Alice invited them both to sit and waited. At last the man spoke.

"Excuse the liberty, Missus," he began. "You've been more than fair to Rob here; he thinks the world of you. And kind to the wife. It seems like there's no-one in this town – and I've lived here all my life... I've not been to work today... been down the nick since yesterday teatime. They've given him police bail now for a bit."

"Is there no solicitor or someone of that nature at the police station whose duty it is to support you?" enquired Alice. "I really know nothing about such matters."

Mr. Little snorted. "Support nothing," he said. "Stopped the both of us from saying anything to put things right, he did, and then told us on the quiet to admit to everything and make it out it was horse play that went wrong."

"But I never done nothing, Miss! I swear on my mother's..."

"That will do, Rob," said Alice hastily. She had learned enough lately not to risk further enlargement of her vocabulary for a while. "It is unnecessary for you to swear. We both know you were cruel to the poor boy who was killed..."

"Miss! Miss! You know all about that, I told you, we never meant him no harm, not real harm like."

"True. And after that conversation I am quite sure you had nothing to do with his death. But you called him some very bad names. Many people are aware of that and that is why they suspect you. Why did you hate him so?"

"Miss, we never. It was only a bit of fun. He was only a poof, miss."

"That about 'queerbashers' in the paper, it was all bollocks," said Mr. Little. "Excuse my language, Missus. I think

I've gone a bit mental the way things are. These kids, they don't know half what they think they do. It's just words to them."

"Sticks and stone may break your bones but words will never hurt you," murmured Alice.

"That's about the size of it, Missus."

"You don't need to convince me, Mr. Little. I was already certain your son was innocent of this crime and am very anxious indeed that the true perpetrator should be apprehended, but I am at a loss to know what I can do about it."

"It all happened the day you had that burglar, Missus, and our lad and his mates took you down the nick. If you can remind the sergeant of that. Then the lads came straight home to tell us. They was full of it, dancing about. They never went out again that night, I swear. It's their alibi."

"If you think it would be of any help, I will certainly do so. But the police do know all that already, if, as I assume, you have informed them of the boys' whereabouts after they left me at the police station."

"Anything you can do, Missus, we'd be ever so grateful. I don't know where to turn and that's the truth. I can tell you, it's a great thing just to be believed."

She watched them go, the man's protective arm round his son's shoulders. Then she went straight to ring Peter.

Chapter Twelve

Alice recounted her day's adventures to Peter over the phone.

"Don't be carried away by compassion, my dear," he counselled her. "How would you expect any family to react? In the face of public hostility they close ranks, don't they? It becomes a black-and-white them-and-us situation. Don't forget this is their boy and anything he does or is perceived to do reflects upon them. Of course they insist on and probably even believe in his innocence. It doesn't prove a thing."

In vain she described Mrs. Little's transparent distress. The woman had just been subjected to a horrific example of mass ostracism, he pointed out, with the inevitable result. As for the father's behaviour, it was no doubt consistent with an honest responsible attitude, but equally so with an experienced working man's guarded negotiating stance.

"He may have very little actual knowledge of his son," he said. "Rob seems to spend most of his time out with his friends looking for mischief and very little at home."

"But if you could have seen them together," said Alice lamely.

"Giving you a good impression."

"No, Peter, no, after they had left too, when they did not know I was watching. He had his arm round Rob, who was leaning against him so trustingly as they walked away, like a little child."

"Under conditions of great stress, don't forget. The family reputation, indeed its whole well-being, is at stake."

She reminded him of how the boys had reacted to the news of Stephen's death, only to have her view of it turned on its head. If they had indeed been responsible for it, he argued, it would have been at least as much of a shock to them to hear it was regarded as murder - they would have realised that it might be traced to them - and he reminded her that she had said that they cheered up when they remembered the paper had referred to it as a drug-induced suicide. Of course they would - it let them off the hook. As to that headline and Nesta's puzzling failure to explain it, Peter paid her the compliment of giving her a delicate but perfectly clear explanation. Alice was amazed. The whole notion of sex was a minefield she had been escorted round with many a dark warning by her mother in her youth and had since prudently skirted. "I have not really come to terms with my own conception yet," she admitted, ruefully, "when I think of my father and mother - oh dear - but as for this!" The Oscar Wilde subject had been so excoriated by her father that she had hardly been aware of a sexual connotation at all. "It buggers belief. Oh! - Have I not just slipped into another of those words I must not use?"

"Yes, careful, Alice," he said, affectionately. "Words again. Another name for the people we are talking about is 'buggers'."

He could almost hear the sound of pennies dropping in the ensuing silence.

"And these children know all about that too?"

"Or do they? Only enough to use it as a hate concept, a battle cry, I suspect."

That must have been what Rob's father meant. 'They are only words to them'. Words, words, how dangerous they could be after all, especially to those like herself unaware of their own ignorance. Never mind sticks and stones, they could only break your bones, words could destroy you utterly. Could the boys have been right about Stephen? Could Stephen really have behaved in this, frankly disgusting, manner? Peter gently pointed out that they had no evidence either way, even if it had mattered, and that Rob and his friends probably hadn't either, but although she might think of these youths as children, physically they were coming into their sexual prime and were likely to be more excited by it than that at any other time in their lives. But even if it had been - what had Peter just called it? - Stephen's 'sexual orientation' - and she found it deeply difficult to believe - why should anyone, let alone young boys, want to kill him for it?

"You would never look at the tabloids, of course, but more serious papers? Television? I suppose what you neither understand nor like the sound of you just skip."

She nodded, not proud of herself. "Indeed, that has been the case for many years. As for television, I have never possessed a set. But I do want to understand, Peter," she said, humbly.

So he told her about some of the high profile cases of homosexuals, some of them famous artists or actors, who had been abused and murdered by ignorant bigoted people. "You see, my dear, it has proved a sufficient motive in the past, especially where a single individual has been set upon by a mob. And adolescent boys can work each other up into a frenzy of excitement. Girls too, I wouldn't wonder. Intoxicated by their own hormones, dear lady, believe me."

"Peter, are telling me you think it is possible...?"

"That Stephen was a homosexual? Or that these lads are capable of killing him or anyone else for that or any other reason? Possible, yes, I do think so, either or both of those things."

"But Peter, surely you cannot believe..."

"My dear Alice, we simply don't have enough evidence in either case to make a judgement. What Stephen was in this respect really doesn't matter. As for whether his death was brought about by Rob and his friends, it has to be properly investigated before it can be ruled out."

Alice was mutinous. It was their first disagreement and opened a small but chill rift between them. She tried another angle. "It is not only these families I am worried about," she reflected. "I also worry about Stephen's family. You did say the police had traced them and that the father had been down, but by now the mother must be back from her holiday. She will have had the news and be desperate to know more. I know I would. I would like to be able to tell her that his last words were so loving and so concerned for her."

Peter gratefully received this little olive branch, but could not in conscience accept it in a positive spirit. "A bit difficult, I'm afraid. Understandably the police are, to use Cornford's own expression, 'playing hard to get' about names and addresses."

Alice mutinied again. "It is not at all understandable to

me. I am certain that nasty reporter would obtain them in a flash."

"But then you wouldn't know whether to trust the information or not, would you," countered Peter. "And if we were ever to approach him, he'd smell a story and never leave us alone."

"I have no intention of approaching him. I have a much better idea." She reminded him how Stephen's main subjects at school had been English. He must have made a great impression on his English teacher, a gifted boy like that - he had mentioned a Mrs. Holmes, or a Mrs. Watson, it would come back to her, she was sure. A lady of whom he thought very highly, as she recalled. A teacher like that would be certain to remember his poetry, would be interested in his pitiful story, would want to do anything she could to help. Lestrange, that was it, Betty Lestrange.

"So you want me to write to Ms. B. Lestrange, private and personal, at which school do you think?"

"Try them all. Put a return address on the back of the envelope. The worst they can do is send it back, is it not? - Oh Peter, it is so good of you."

Peter shook his head a little dubiously, but he was happy again. This was after all, a positive step and one they could take in harmony.

Chapter Thirteen

Peter's letters were in the post box on Thursday morning. One of them should reach the target by Friday, the mail permitting; at the very earliest a reply could not be expected before Monday. By tacit consent, after a brief call to report what he had done, he and Alice made no contact over the weekend. She and Nesta decided to go to the cinema on Saturday, something Alice had very rarely done since the odd chaperoned excursion to see her idol, Fred Astaire, in her youth. The Playhouse was doing a return showing of 'Shakespeare In Love'.

"You'll find it educational," said Nesta, twinkling.

"Oh yes, I am sure I will. I love Shakespeare," agreed Alice with enthusiasm, "though I have never seen any of the film versions. Nor indeed any version at all since a very long time ago, when father was able to take me to the Stratford Memorial Theatre."

"Not educational in that sense. Not a play by him. About him. Very modern approach. You'll see."

She did see. And was very much astonished and considerably uncomfortable. "I suppose it is a very clever play," she conceded bravely. "I recognised a great many references to his work. Do you think," she asked, guardedly, "that Shakespeare and his circle actually did behave like that?"

"Welcome to the world, my love. - Be nice to have Daphne back, eh? Coming home late Monday, remember? Might be too tired for class Tuesday morning of course."

"I do hope she comes," replied Alice, her thoughts elsewhere. She devoted her Sunday morning to overdue housework, having abandoned the strict sabbatarian regime espoused by her parents.

The phone rang before nine o'clock on Monday morning. "How about coffee at the Rose?" Peter asked. "I've got a letter to show you."

"Oh Peter, how wonderful. At any rate, I hope it is. But not the Rose, it makes me too sad."

"Make it the Ottakars Bookshop cafe then," he suggested. "Ten thirty too soon?"

She was already waiting for him when he worked his buggy through the automatic doors and found his way to the table near the entrance she had earmarked for them. He took the letter out and handed it to her.

Dear Mr. Ratcliffe,

It read,

I cannot tell you how shocked I was to receive your letter. Such a brilliant boy. I had been puzzled and somewhat hurt not to have heard from him after the examination results came out, though of course I had only taught him up to GCSE level, when he left our school for the Sixth Form College. He should have been at Cambridge by now; with four grade As at A Level, two of them starred, plus a top grade in his Latin, he had more than met the conditions for the place he had been offered at Kings College. I am at a loss to know what he was doing in Weston-super-Mare instead of being in Cambridge, where I fully believed he had gone, or why his name should have been unknown at the time and place of his dreadful death. It would be a great kindness on your part if you would tell me more about the last days of this tragic young person, of such shining promise so cruelly wasted.

His name was Stephen Venables, not a pupil any teacher would be able to forget. I'm afraid at the moment I am unable to recall his address in Woodley, but when I have had a chance to look it up in the school's records on Monday I will let you know.

In deep distress, Yours, Betty Lestrange.

"So that's what his plans were," said Peter. "No wonder he held them so close to his heart. What he was waiting for was the passport to Cambridge and the literary career he dreamed of."

"Oh Peter, all that work, and all those hopes, to end like that..."

"Kicked like a dog and thrown into the sea," said Peter bitterly, and instantly regretted it. He put an arm round her shaking shoulders.

Darren Vowles, over an espresso at the next table, had stopped scribbling to listen.

Alice was openly weeping now. "To think of it," she managed to say, "top grades in all those subjects - and he never knew -"

"English Lit. and Lang., Psychology and Spanish, wasn't it?"

"And the Latin too."

"Kings would be very glad to get him, with a record like that. I wonder what they made of his failure to claim his place."

"Excuse me," said Darren, coming over, the picture of sympathetic concern, "I could hardly help overhearing. Are you by any chance talking about the young man who was sent to his death so tragically at Anchor Head?"

"And who are you?" demanded Peter.

Darren produced his press card, in his persona of serious professional man.

"May I suggest you mind your own business," observed Peter, affably.

"Pardon me sir, this is what my business is," riposted Darren and bowed himself rapidly away.

Inevitably the resultant piece in the following morning's Post was eagerly discussed at Nesta's class. Alice remained silent. She had hardly brought herself to go at all and devoutedly wished now that she had not.

"Absolutely appalling," declared Nesta at large. "Such a promising young life..." (To whom you once attributed 'whingeing beggary' and 'dirty needles', Alice could not but silently remind herself.) "...snuffed out by a bunch of mindless criminals."

Alice's restraint gave way. "Now, Nesta, how can you say that? They are only children, high-spirited children, Rob and his chums." She was remembering her own passionate tears when she had felt her child self unjustly accused by her father, before she had learned from Charlotte Bronte to 'bow to the storm without breaking'. Even now it was hard to forgive her beloved Mummy, who had never interceded for her, just wept quietly.

Daphne giggled. Alice glared at her.

"Alice darling, you're gorgeous! Not 'chums', sweetie, that goes right back before the war."

Alice was disconcerted. "What then? 'Pals'?"

"That's back to the first war, ducky, straight out of Henty and Ballantyne and The Boys Own."

"Oh." Alice had lived a vicarious childhood through her father's shelves of those very authors and bound magazines. "What does it matter what I call them?" She was tetchy. "You do not know those boys are guilty. All the evidence is circumstantial. And they have an alibi."

Daphne was suddenly avidly interested. "Something I don't know about?" she demanded.

Nesta looked blank for a moment, then, "Of course, missed all the excitement. Tramping all over Cyprus at the time, lucky so-and-so. Must've wondered what we were all on about. Have to bring you up to speed." So she did.

"I knew about the boy falling off the cliff, of course. That was the night we three old bags had been on the spree and my cousin arrived before we got back." She gave Alice a conspiratorial wink. "So he was murdered, was he? I thought the consensus was he'd chucked himself over under the influence. And so now it turns out he was a model student just off to Cambridge. Wow! What I want to know in that case is why he was begging in our High Street, getting material for a book or what?"

"Nobody knows why he was here," put in Alice.

Tongues were loosened: "You missed the house to house then -" "- great excitement-" "- all had to account for our movements that night -" "- as if anyone like us could possibly have been -" "- lots of evidence about those dreadful yobs -" "- that Alice calls 'Rob's pals' -" ("Alice, you do make some funny friends" - "Hark who's talking!")

"Alice hit the nail. All circumstantial. General behaviour," boomed Nesta judicially, remembering Alice's sensitivity on this score. "Nothing to connect them with this particular evening."

"Oh but there was." Daphne looked as shocked as her hearers. "I never gave it a thought till now, but then, I'd no idea it was a murder, had I."

"Come on Daph. Spit it out."

"I recall it quite clearly. It was such a wonderful sunset that night - we saw it beginning as we came home, Nesta, you remember - I took my cousin up to the Head to see it. It was pretty much over by the time we got up there, must've been three quarters of an hour later or more. All we saw was the afterglow and the moon coming up. My cousin loved it, wanted to know why we were bothering to go all the way to Cyprus."

"And ?"

"That little gang was up there then. I heard shouting and scuffling and all in a moment they came bursting up the steps at the end of your block, Alice, you know how they do, and ran down the road as if the devil were after them, looking back over their shoulders as they went. Beryl would tell you, my cousin, the one who went on the walking thing with me, she'd tell you. We didn't think anything of it at the time. Well, would you. Kids!"

Nesta called off her class and drove Daphne to the police station. "Sorry, old thing," she whispered to Alice as they left. "Gone for a burton, that alibi. Want to come?" But Alice didn't; she felt too bruised and exhausted.

The incident room leapt into renewed activity. All the gang were brought in once more for questioning, convoyed navy fashion by some of their fathers. Faced with the new evidence Rob was very frightened and showed it. So was Mr. Little, though he didn't, except to the experienced eye that was upon him.

"I'll tell you the truth," said the boy, with an imploring look at his father.

"About time," said Sergeant Hopsack, gently. "Go on then."

"We was along there all right, we was picking up our lines, but it wasn't that Stephen we was having a rumble with. We never seen him that night. It was that bloody man."

"Right," said the sergeant, kindly as ever, "what man

was that then?"

"That man the old lady was on about - dead scared she was - you remember, you was there at the nick when we brought her along -"

"See, would they have come near you lot if they just done a murder - were just going to do -"

"That's enough, Mr. Little, let the boy speak for himself."

"We thought it must be him."

"You didn't recognise him then?"

"We never seen him, did we! Not then. No sign of him when she come rushing out. Honest to God, we thought she was off her trolley, poor old cow, we never seen no man after her. But when we seen him that night we knew it was him, all glaring eyes and teeth like she said, only in the dark, and jumping like the devil, I mean, what was he doing hanging about there in the dark? He wanted to know about a boy who was living round there he said, and we laughed and said we didn't know any boys round there, only old bags - well, Miss Fairbairn's a real nice old lady, but we didn't tell him about her, no fear - and he swore at us and waved his arms about, so we swore at him and he went for us and we ran away. It was dead scary. No blame to the old lady being frightened. He had like a white face and fucking big spiky eyebrows. Like a devil. We ran like stink and never seen him no more after we got to the road, see." Rob was beginning to enjoy himself. "Heard him shouting at someone, though. We went for some chips at that place down the front and played football on the beach for a bit, to give him a chance to clear off, and then we went back to get our lines up, dead quiet in case he was still hanging around. But he weren't. And the tide had come in - we never did get our lines up that night, did we."

"Why did you tell us you were home all evening?"

"You weren't never going to believe us, were you! You never believed the old lady, did you?"

"Where did you get that idea?"

"Fucking obvious weren't it."

After a while the boys were given bail again and then the whole incident room relaxed into laughter, with a feeling that the end game had begun. Someone drew a highly imaginative 'identikit picture' of the man with the spiky black eyebrows and glaring eyes and snarling teeth and they all clustered round the board to admire it.

"Better put the frighteners on those lying parents," said Sergeant Hopsack.

WPC Sandra Shepherd, who had been made family liaison officer for the investigation, stood contemplating the drawing. A statuesque young woman, her poised stillness among the bustle at the end of the working day caught the sergeant's attention. He looked from the flawless oval of her face, fine black brows drawn down in a thoughtful line, to the caricature on the board and back again.

"Recognise him or something, Sand?"

She shook her head and smiled. (Stunning looker that one, he registered absently.) "Of course not, Sarge. I wasn't looking at that, just thinking."

"Penny for 'em." Hopsack returned to clearing his desk of litter.

"Well," she said, slowly, "thank God we've got this thing pretty fairly wrapped up now."

"Yeah. Go on then."

"Oh, sweet, Sarge! 'Go on then' he says, so gentle, and they cough. OK, here it is. I've not been perfectly happy about that family set-up in Stoke. Fair enough when it was only identification. But when it turns out it was foul play, isn't it a bit strange I've never seen the victim's mother, only the stepfather?"

"I thought she'd gone on a touring holiday with some mates?"

"I only had his word for it though. Seemed fair enough at the time, as I say, it was only an identification and I could understand him wanting to break the news to her himself. Seemed pretty upset about it himself, shattered, and about the boy running off in the first place, back in July, too. All as per normal family. But when I went up to tell them it was foul play I still didn't see her. Out at work, he told me, very vague about where. Couldn't give me an address or a phone number for it."

"I know. You put it in your report."

"Anyone been in touch with Woodley about that?"

"What do you think? We morons or something? But events down here have stolen a march on us."

"Right enough. Sorry, Sarge. Great we're getting it sewn up so quickly."

"But it still bothers you," he observed, slamming the last drawer shut. The glow of her smile lit her face into eloquent beauty. He gave it a try. "How about a swift half up Status Four ?"

"No, Sarge, thanks all the same, I'm off out to dinner with Robert. - Look, you've still got that grease spot on your tie from yesterday's chips - Noreen slipping?"

Slap on the wrist for me, thought Hopsack, and locked up.

Chapter Fourteen

In the face of Peter's scepticism about her championship of Rob and his friends, Alice found the breaking of their alibi too painful a shock for her to want to tell him about it. She had to address the turmoil in her mind and try and make sense of it first, so that she could break the news in the most truthful way. Peter, however, heard it from Nesta, whom he almost literally ran into when he negotiated the corner of the High Street in his buggy just as she came sailing round it in the opposite direction. There was no possibility of avoiding a social encounter.

"My apologies, dear lady. I trust you are not injured."

"Tut tut, Mr. Ratcliffe. Ought to nick you for dangerous driving - or is it drunk in charge? No, too early no doubt. Seriously, no harm done. Scarcely touched me. Took the wind out of my sails. Nothing at all."

"May I ask you to join me in a pot of Earl Grey to restore your composure?"

"Heavens! No need for that!"

"The least I can do. If you have the time, that is." He hoped in vain that she had not. Avoiding both the Rose and Ottakars, he escorted her into the Pickwick, which involved considerable manoeuvres with his chair. Finally it had to be left on the pavement, while he lumbered in on his two sticks. She was a graceful woman, in spite of her bulk and appalling dress sense, he reflected, as she accommodated herself on too small a chair, her sturdy skirt riding up above her formidable knees.

"Seen our little mutual friend lately? Mmmm? Up to speed on the saga of her tragic young protégé?" Brushing aside his murmured response she went on, "Quite a drama in my class this morning - do a history group for the U3A for my sins, into the Glorious Revolution and all that jazz, Whigs and Tories and

Jacobites, great stuff - No, that wasn't the drama. No. Turns out those young thugs who mugged Alice did the dirty deed. Alibi's busted. Spotted practically red-handed by friend Daphne. Just surfaced, Daphne - been walkabout abroad - Ha! That's good! Walkabout it was, hills in Cyprus, lucky so-and-so. And guess what?"

Peter raised a benign eyebrow.

"Our Alice goes and gets all passionate in their defence! Would you credit that?"

His face was bland. "Yes, I would credit that."

"Poor old duck, doesn't know her way around. Like a child, vulnerable. Know what? I blame that mummy and daddy of hers."

"She loves them still, you know."

"Kindness to be cruel, I call it. Imprisonment in the name of protection. Comes into the real world at the age of nearly seventy. Like an alien. No defences, no strategies. God help her if a con man lights on her. Easy meat."

"Heaven forfend," he murmured.

"Dam' good, these shortbreads."

"Have another."

"Shouldn't - ah well, too late to worry about my weight. Husband didn't like it. Too bad, gone now. Cirrhosis. Like the Yorkshireman of whom someone asked had he died and got the answer: 'Nay, I couldn't rightly say but us burnt him on t'spec this afternoon.'" She laughed explosively and the point of the story was lost in a shower of crumbs. "Ah well... Alice now, subject of marriage, absolute scream. Utopia no less! What does she know? Ah well, bless her innocent heart. - How was yours? Marriage? Hmmm?"

Peter blinked. Annie's face swam into his mind, blanked out or twisted into slyness by Alzheimer's. How dared this woman call up that image?

"Sorry. Sorry. Gone too far. Not the first time. None of my business. Sorry. No hard feelings?"

"Of course not."

She rose. "Thanks for the tea. And the shortbreads. Wicked, but who cares. Dear Alice. Values your friendship, you know."

"Yours too." He was glad to be able to say as much with sincerity. "Forgive me for not getting up." He watched her stately progress up the street. She was right; Alice was a lamb among wolves. Blast those bloody parents, he thought, in a flash of irritation. How could they make her so defenceless? Yet that was just what so endeared her, her innocence, coupled with her strong sense of injustice and determination to stand up for the underdog. The trouble was that her judgement was so unbalanced, so wanting the ballast of experience. She had been right about the lad Stephen, true, but these young hooligans? It overstretched belief... He must protect her from herself. But wasn't that just what her parents thought they were doing?

Nesta forged up the hill towards her apartment block like a galleon in the Trades, but she was not quiet in her mind. She'd blown it again. Such a nice man, too, and Alice's friend. Anything in that? she wondered. Alice? Why not? Wasted on Alice, she reflected ruefully. A real gentleman in the good old-fashioned sense - term of abuse these days, like 'lady', sad that - but someone who would take responsibility. Not, she surmised, a man who would womanise or drink or anything else to excess. Not someone who would remortgage the house behind his wife's back and then go and die on her, leaving her with nothing but awesome debts. She allowed herself a moment of regret for the shining promise of Ed's youth, the riotous success of that first book, how lucky she and everyone who knew them thought she had been to net him. A golden couple! Ha! And how it was only later she came to understand the true nature of that luck. Her bitten lips narrowed to a tight line. Then she straightened up, took a deep breath and, lengthening her stride, deliberately relaxed. Steady the Buffs, she scolded herself.

Alice had employed the afternoon in going for a walk into town, along Beach Road, round the whole sickle of the bay and back through the parks and gardens. It might have been Shepherds Bush to Clapham Common for all the notice she took of it. Cutting through Grove Park at the end was a mistake though. It was the scene of her first encounter with Rob and his friends. Their whole saga came flooding back and she was buffeted by warring emotions. The gloomy day had darkened into deep dusk and she was tired by the time she got home. She hesitated by the telephone, but easily persuaded herself that she needed a cup of tea first. Before she had finished the pot it was time for the six o'clock news. And then the Debussy on Radio Four she had been looking forward to. She looked at the telephone again and stood poised. No, she was hungry now; it could wait until she had prepared and eaten her supper.

It was gone nine before she gave herself a shake and made purposefully for the phone at last. It rang just as she reached it. She picked it up.

"Peter!" she laughed, out of breath. "I was on the point of ringing you" - and have been for ten hours, as she did not say - "and then I was afraid nine o'clock was perhaps too late."

"Late as it is, I have news for you, my dear. I tried more than once earlier, but there was no answer. I very much fear your faith in human nature has to take another knock. The police have blown that alibi to smithereens. Those boys were seen very near the scene of the crime again after dark that night. It was not true that having gone home after leaving you at the police station they had stayed there the whole evening."

She was silent, her news pulled out from under feet.

"Don't be too upset, Alice. Not all your ugly ducklings can turn out to be swans, you know. Don't let it stop you from seeing the best in everyone; it often does bring that very thing out in them."

A deep sob reached him along the wires.

"Oh, come on, old girl, brace up."

Her voice choked between a laugh and a sob. "You sound like Nesta," she said.

He did not mention having bumped into that lady. "And you sound extremely upset."

"I cannot believe those children did this terrible thing."

"Someone did it. And the professionals think they are the culprits. Don't you want Stephen's killers caught and punished?"

"Yes, of course. But the right ones. Not these boys. I cannot believe - I cannot bring myself to believe it of them. I have been thinking about it all day and the more I contemplate the possibility the more preposterous it seems. Yes, indeed."

"Rob had lied to you, Alice, and so had his father." He sounded exasperated.

"I know, I know." She sounded as though she were wringing her hands. "Peter, I have this strong feeling that I must speak to Stephen's mother. He did love her, you know. We need to talk about him, she and I. After all," she went on, lamely, "I was the last person to whom her son spoke. And of her."

"Time was when I would have taken you up to Stoke to see her, as soon as Mrs. Lestrange comes up with the address," he reflected bitterly. "Now I can't even get up to your flat."

"Oh my dear Peter," she said, wistfully, "I wish I had met you when you were young."

"Ah yes," he responded, mischievously, "but by the time you had left school I was already a married man."

She was glad he could not see her flaming face. "You know that was not at all what I meant." She could not tell him how much she would have liked to superimpose the image of the tall vigorous man he must have been upon his aged self, still in his way handsome, but oh so bent and frail.

"You meant you'd rather see someone other than a useless old hulk." The chuckle had quite gone. His voice was raw.

"Oh no, that is very far from what - you are not - Oh dear, I really did not mean-"

"I know what you really meant. When you're in a hole, Alice, don't dig."

The blood beating in her ears sounded like heavy doors thudding shut down the echoing length of the wires. The silence weighed unbearably. Finally, furtively, she laid the phone down. After another long pause she heard the click of the receiver rest at the other end, the last door shutting. She replaced her own receiver and went early to bed, feeling more wretchedly alone than she had since the first little while after her mother's death, worse than then, because she had since discovered what it was to have a real friend. And now she had thrown that friendship away. She remembered she still had a few of those sleeping pills her doctor had given her when her mother died and she took one, reckless of whether or not it had passed its use-by date. As she tucked her hot bottle into the most comforting inner curve of her foetal sleeping position, she admonished herself; she was so fortunate, she had so many friends now, not like then, so many...Hours later she surfaced, fighting the rags of a nightmare. Its howls and shrieks slowly gave way to the sounds of the sea hissing and dragging on the rocks below. The huge-eyed wide-mouthed faces struggling in the waters of her dream shrank and whispered away into the edges of the dark, where they popped into oblivion like blown grape pips. Blinking thankfully into full wakefulness, she decided to make herself some herbal tea. Half past three; the heating had been off for six hours. Clutching her fleecy dressing gown round her, she took her tray back to bed and snuggled back in to drink her tea. Just as well to stay awake for a little, she thought. She had no wish to be ensnared in the same dream again.

  Waking thoughts, however, were little better. She knew she had, as Nesta would put it, 'blown it'. It was true she had many friends these days, more correctly termed 'friendly acquaintances' perhaps, but no longer anyone to confide in, no-one to listen with understanding to her vehement conviction that the police were barking up the wrong tree. Least of all the police themselves, who had long ago written her off as a harmless case of incipient senile dementia. Or Peter, who... Oh, what had she done? ... Oh dear, these miserable people, they had lied, they had lied to her, she who was convinced of their innocence and only wanted to help. Why did she feel so strongly, even in the face of all the lies, that the boys had been guilty of nothing so wicked? Had she forgotten what Stephen had previously suffered from them, what he had suffered since? Oh poor boy, poor dear boy, he never knew how very well he had done. He could have been in Cambridge now, where Peter's sons had gone. If he could only have confided in her, Peter might have been able to sort it all out and he would have been there now. And safe, happy and safe. If only - if only -

  Of all people she had not intended to hurt Peter. How could she have been so insensitive? That came of thinking too much upon her own troubles. Selfish, selfish. He would never forgive her now. Yet she had been able to talk to him as she had never been able to talk to anyone, even (and that only when she was little and never in later life) her own dear mother.

Had Stephen been able to talk to his mother? His last thoughts were of her, so pitiful. Alice shied away from the memory like a seared hand from a hot iron. His murderer must be caught, must not be allowed to hide behind wrongful convictions, to allow Rob and his chu.. his pa.., those other boys to be his scapegoats. Which in the end is worse, leaving a crime unpunished or condemning the wrong people? She could not know - "Oh yes I do," she cried aloud into the shadowy bedroom, "because either way the criminal escapes and to penalise the innocent doubles the injustice! I should never have gone on urging the police into action!" In her mind she was still seeking Peter's support, blaming herself, hoping for him to contradict her: if she had only done more for Stephen this would never have happened, he might have been in Cambridge; if only she had not reported the boys' behaviour in Grove Park, so self-righteous, they might never have been the focus of suspicion; if only she had not insisted so obstinately about the blood; if only she had left it to Captain Gilford and the professionals as they had all told her she should - maybe Stephen would still have been alive - maybe so many people would not have had their lives destroyed. How she yearned for Peter to soothe away her self doubt, as once he had done.

'My dear Alice,' he had said, 'remember what Stephen told you himself, that you were the kindest person he had ever met. All you have done at any point was for the best and most caring of motives. But,' he had added, 'the police are not fools; they have accepted your evidence and are working on it very professionally, I assure you. They will establish the truth in time.' But that is what she still doggedly refused to put any trust in. Now she no longer had Peter to lean on, she had to stand alone.

Round and round in her head it went, as she pulled her blankets up close and poured herself another cup of camomile tea. It was stewed and cold. She peered at the clock, nearly twenty past five. Might as well get my breakfast, she thought wryly. She was not going to be able to sleep again that night.

She turned her little blow heater on rather than overriding the central heating timer, and brought her tray of cereal and a fresh pot of tea back to bed too.

Those unhappy children! She could never feel about them as she felt about Stephen. He was - had been, so special a person. But the misery and lovingness of their parents, liars though they had proved to be, had touched her heart. As for the boys, rough, ignorant, thoughtless, liars too, all this they certainly were, but murderers? Their lives were going to be ruined for ever if the real killer were not apprehended. How much harm had already been irreversibly done to their characters? She could see Peter was right; their involvement had to be thoroughly investigated before they could be cleared of suspicion. But what if the investigation stopped at this point, as it looked only too likely to do? The inspector was in full cry after his quarry, nothing would please him more than to conclude his case nicely and quickly (and cheaply too, she thought, cynically - however had she become so cynical?) never mind that all those families would be destroyed, not to mention Stephen's reputation being left in tatters (Peter's explanation of that 'queer bashers' headline was still ricocheting around in her head, causing her to think of Oscar Wilde with a new and horrified insight. Such a brilliant intellect too!) Someone was going to have to look elsewhere for the perpetrator and, if not herself, who was there who would?

Oh, Peter - Peter -

Where should she look? Then she remembered 'Oh Miss, my poor Mum' and heard it with fresh ears. Stephen had clearly loved his mother very much and yet he had left home. Whatever had happened there that was so desperately bad that it had driven him to the degradation of the streets? The secret must lie there. And he had been afraid for his mother - 'my poor mum'. Why? She must talk to the woman at all costs, for clearly no-one else was going to do it. Did the poor soul even know her son's fate? If she did, why had she not been down, if only for the identification? 'Touring holiday' indeed!

She dressed herself in the lovat kilt and jumper from Heather Valley and the green anorak Daphne had persuaded her to buy (such a practical garment, so light and warm) tidied everything away, turned down the central heating thermostat, locked up dutifully and went out into the chill to get the car. It was still dark.

Chapter Fifteen

Alice's nightmare was thus followed in short order by the waking one of her journey north. In forty years of unblemished driving (her competence in this being one of her father's insurances against his own old age) she had rarely driven in the dark and never on a motorway, there being in fact only just over five thousand miles on her ancient Mini's clock. The first spectral image in her mirror after she had crept with trepidation into the inner lane of the M5 was of a white-eyed monster, a vast shape picked out by tiny lights. Its looming closeness and shouldering bow wave of air as it passed went near to unnerving her totally, but, doggedly averting her eyes from the tempting escape offered by the first slip road, to Clevedon, she gradually became more and more able to endure such terrors. When a rather smaller, slower, less intimidating lorry went past, she accelerated to a brave fifty and proceeded at an even distance behind him, like an imprinted duckling. As the traffic built up and the daylight brightened, she began to regard this lorry as a benign if oblivious protector and felt progressively less threatened by the rush and flash of everything else on the road. By the time it left her for Gloucester, an irrational feeling of abandonment soon gave way to an almost nonchalant command of her special territory, the inside lane, where for long periods she reigned alone, careless of the hustle of the outside lanes.

This increasing confidence, however, released her to brood about her problems. She went over and over the events and emotions of yesterday, that had led up to her taking the decision she was now perilously implementing, though she was less and less sure why. The traffic grew ever thicker; she felt like a buffalo calf swept willy nilly along in the skirts of a stampede, quite helpless to do anything but continue, pressured into a speed she had never before done and emphatically did not want to do now, or ever. When at last, for some reason unfathomable to her, the general speed relented, lorries closed up behind, in front and alongside her. Her chest tightened, her face felt cold, her finger tips, clamped to the wheel, were tingling. Take deep slow breaths, Alice, she admonished herself, in her mother's tones; ladies do not panic. She obediently took deep slow breaths and her panic duly diminished. Locked between her guardian lorries she stopped and started, conscientiously moving up and down the gears for what might have been hours (and was certainly miles) before, much to her astonishment, being insinuated into an equally inexorable weight of crawling traffic from the right. The intimate grip of her mighty escort relaxed, space opened round her, she began to feel a little more in control of her own progression, but also rather hungry and alone and unsure of what on earth she was doing there. What had she to say to this woman, Stephen's mother, that would be of the least use to either of them? How was she to find her in the first place? She had overlooked the fact that she had not yet received the address from Mrs. Lestrange. 'Stephen Venables' mother, present name and address unknown, Stoke-on-Trent,' was not going to get her very far - though it had, she reminded herself with a precarious giggle, already brought her rather a long way. Her only recourse was to find the school and ask for Mrs. Betty Lestrange. Would the school people mind? Oh silly, silly Alice. Her petrol was getting low. She must find a garage and then perhaps it would be best to turn round and go home. How did one turn round on these great unforgiving roads? When she had done so, there was the prospect of that terrible junction in reverse. She supposed. And shuddered.

Unexpectedly, down a swinging downhill curve, she saw and thankfully followed great blue signs for Stoke and, crossing the motorway bridge, entered a cutting lined with lorries in long laybies on either hand. She pulled in behind one and sat shaking with relief, head bowed over the steering wheel.

"You all right, Missus?" enquired a friendly northcountry voice. There were two bright eyes in a square stubbled face peering in at her. "Want some help? Come far?"

"Weston-super-Mare."

"Long way for a lady that's, excuse me, not so young as

she was. You sure you're all right? You look proper poorly. Tell you what, you'll feel a lot better for a bite to eat and a cuppa. They make us professionals take a break, tha knows. Matter of fact, that's what we're all doing here. Look, I've got a drop of tea left in my flask - how about a cup?" Alice was truly touched. She wound her window down and, eyes glistening, put out a grateful hand. "Many thanks indeed, but I think I will press on to Stoke. Then I will take your excellent advice and look for something to eat as soon as I get there. I only hope I am on the right road. Is it far?"

"Nay. Straight on, follow the signs, you can't go wrong. Cheerio then."

She smiled and waved at him as he climbed back into his cab. What a lot of very kind people there were in the world, she told herself, gratefully. She had forgotten to put on her watch and the car clock could not possibly be right. If it was she had been over six hours on the road; no wonder she was tired and hungry.

Peter shuffled along his hall, picked up his post with his long-handled gripper and took it back to his breakfast table. There was a letter from Mrs. Lestrange giving him Stephen's Stoke address and the name of the stepfather, Wayne Blackmore. Better ring Alice; he was glad of an excuse to do so. He had not had a good night; unable to put their strained phone call out of his mind, he had rehearsed its details endlessly in the dark. She had been so upset. His crass joke about the missed opportunities of their youth had misfired unforgivably. He was mortified by that and exceedingly galled by his own incapacity to give practical help. Such an innocent, such a good woman, she was ready to see the best in everyone, resolutely unwilling to believe the worst. Was this the result of her sheltered life or of sheer native goodness? One thing he was certain of, whether or not that impossible woman was right about Alice's parents - and he rather thought she was - her loving trust in them must never be undermined. She was like a nun, emerging into the world after a lifetime enclosed, amazed and delighted and concerned and, as far as he could see, absolutely unembittered by what she found she had lost. A precious person. She was so sure of the innocence of her young thugs; was it possible that those clear blue eyes saw something that was hidden from others?

He rang her number. No reply. She must have gone for her paper.

He went out for his own and chanced upon Cornford in the newsagents. The inspector greeted him cheerfully.

"Good news, sir. Forensics have come up with direct evidence against that little gang. Looks pretty conclusive." He smiled expansively, generous in his consciousness of success. "I do hand it to your little lady friend, I must say. If she hadn't brought up that blood business we'd've had no reason to suspect foul play. Good thing she did. It doesn't do to let kids think they can get away with murder." He caught himself up short. "Especially when it really is murder," he said hastily, adding belatedly, "Or anyone else, come to that."

Peter fished, but was given no details of the new evidence. However, he now had a second piece of news for Alice. He tried the phone again, but without success. Having achieved no response by half past ten he began to worry, cursing himself that he had never remembered to get Nesta's telephone number or even her name. A Freudian forget, no doubt, wretched woman. As once before, he found himself reduced to going round to Alice's flat, though, as he asked himself scoldingly, if she wasn't available to answer the phone, what was the use of struggling up to the door and ringing there? No use at all, was the only answer, but he did establish one disquieting fact; her garage door was swinging in the wind (black mark, old girl, what would your friendly policewoman say?) and her car was gone, for only the second time in a year as far as he was aware. To his relief he saw Nesta turning into the corner of her road as he drove home, only to be dashed to hear that she knew of no reason for Alice's absence.

"Shopping? No? I'll set the old grapevine to work," she promised. "Give you a ring later, What's your number?"

Back home, he went over his last conversation with Alice yet again. 'Peter,' she had said, 'I have this strong feeling I should talk to Stephen's mother' and he had responded only by being angry with himself for his perceived inability to take her. Of course, that was where she had gone. That was why the car was missing. What he had felt to be beyond his own powers she had resolved to do herself, an undertaking, he was sure, far beyond anything she had ever even attempted in the way of driving, never mind having been regularly accustomed to doing it as he had been himself. How he had been put to shame! He cursed himself loud and long.

Then it hit him: Alice was following a hunch again. The reason she was so sure about her young thugs must be that she suspected someone else and that could only be the stepfather. Despairing of anyone else's help, even his - he threw his stick across the room in a fury of frustration - she had gone off on her own to confront the man, right into the dragon's lair. Breathing hard, he rang Cornford. The WPC on the desk told him the inspector was not around. No, she said, smoothly, none of the senior staff were available; could she ask the first one who was to ring Mr. Ratcliffe as soon as possible?

Angry as he was, and he made his feelings abundantly clear, Peter had to settle for that. He made himself some coffee. The phone rang, but it was only Nesta commiserating with him that no-one in any of her numerous circles had any idea where their absurd little friend might be. He tried to console himself that whatever Alice's suspicions were, forensics had come up with clinching evidence against the local suspects. Regardless of what she might think, she was not in fact courting danger.

Or was she?

"My God!" he whispered aloud, aghast. Fool! Fool! Why had it not struck him before? That man, Blackmore, the stepfather, had told the police that he and Stephen's mother had no idea where the boy had been, but they had. It was just within the bounds of belief that Stephen's first letter had gone astray, but they had watched him, he and Alice both, as he had posted letters to the woman on two separate occasions. And these letters had given Alice's own name and address.

He rang the police again, very agitated. "This is important and very urgent," he told the WPC. I don't care who you tell, make it the most senior officer you can track down, but tell someone, NOW, that Miss Fairbairn has gone, off her own bat and alone, to see the mother of the dead boy, Venables, at her address in Stoke-on-Trent. There is very good reason to suppose that the man there, the stepfather, may have been involved in the boy's murder. He certainly lied to the police. So move!"

Fuming with frustration and worried to death, Peter put Mrs Lestrange's latest letter in his pocket, got his car out, filled up at his usual petrol station and broke the speed limit all the way up the M5.

"Sand," said Sergeant Hopsack, putting down the internal phone, "like a nice run out? It's time you put the Venables boy's family in the picture again. Tell them we have suspects who have now been charged with his murder."

"Something new then, Sarge?"

"Yeah, forensics have come up with blood samples from between the pattern of one of young Little's trainer soles - and it's Venables's blood."

"After all this time, Sarge? That kid's been all over since Venables copped it, beach at low tide, you name it. Those trainers were only picked up the other day."

"Ah, but he got new ones the day after. These had gotten too small. Lucky they hadn't been binned."

"His mum had put them by for the next brother down I expect," said Sandra, readying herself for the off. "Poor soul, little did she know." WPC Sandra Shepherd knew about such things.

"Oh, and one more thing, Sand. Our intrepid Miss F. rides again. Old Ratcliffe's just rung in to say she thinks it was Venables's stepdad wot dun it and she's gone off to ask him face to face. So be warned."

He was rewarded by that wondrous smile.

Chapter Sixteen

The one fixed idea in Alice's head when she set off again was to follow those signs to Stoke. She wondered vaguely why all the other places seemed to be off to the left - Newcastle, Newcastle again, Uttoxeter, Derby - so that she ought logically to be going in a huge clockwise circle, and yet the road plunged on ahead, seeming for the most part to soar disdainfully above the scenes of development and dereliction on either side of its sundering passage. Strange, she mused, you must be able to turn right, there are buildings over there - and then noticed the recurring bridges immediately following each fork, realised her error and giggled in private embarrassment. As if in a dream she saw lowering ranks of bottle kilns, like the pictures in long-ago school books; the Potteries of course, she reflected, gratified to have recognised them, but when she looked again, where she had seen them stood a long gleaming structure dominating the landscape, a 'stadium' apparently. For games of some sort? Football? She was not sure. Something is amiss, she thought, biting her lips to steady them.

Then the signs for Stoke ran out, or, to be more exact, a smaller sign for 'Stoke 1/4 mile' pointing off to the left was contradicted by a 'City Centre' one straight ahead. Impatient sounds from behind pushed her into a decision; she went on forward. After all, she needed a post office or a police station to ask for directions and those, she reasoned, were more likely to be found in a centre. But then she lost the signs altogether and was faced with a jumble of anonymous destinations. She must have gone too far - what could she do? She found herself in less and less identifiable areas, diving under railway arches, humping over canal bridges, into a sprawling, multiple-choice roundabout, an ultimate agoraphobic's nightmare. Dithering, startled into a leap forward by infuriated honking from the rear, she threw a wild glance round like a deer in extremis and caught sight of a projecting sign, 'Samaritans', down a side turning. A Good Samaritan was just what she needed. No time to signal her intentions, she wrenched her Mini juddering into the narrow left turn, where with gratitude she edged into the first parking space that offered itself and heaved herself out of the car on to unsteady legs. Blinking to get her bearings, she wandered along the street frontage of a dark brick terrace until she spotted the sign over one of the nondescript doors. She knocked unheard, tried the handle and came into a small entrance lobby with a box office-like window facing her. There was a bell beside it which she pressed. A gently smiling, much wrinkled face appeared behind the glass.

"Hallo, I'm Audrey. Is there something you want to talk about?"

"Yes indeed. Thank you. Not that I am in trouble of any kind, you understand - at any rate, nothing there is any point in burdening you with -"

"I'm here to listen, you know." Audrey had a beautiful quiet smile.

"No, really, I apologise. I ought not to bother you at all, you have so many more important things to do - but I cannot think where to turn for assistance - I have been unable to find a police station or a post office, you see -"

"I could certainly tell you where to find those, but can we do anything for you in the meanwhile?"

"All I need from them is directions, so silly, so sorry to waste your time, I am quite unfamiliar with - I have never been here before - and I need to find -"

"Don't worry. Take your time."

Alice was fumbling in her bag. It slithered out of her fingers like a live thing and fell dead at her feet, spilling its contents. "Oh dear, I am so sorry -" She stooped to gather it up, lurching a little because her head appeared to have a momentum all of its own.

The sweet-voiced lady was out of her box and at her side in half a second. "Are you ill?" she asked, concerned. She sat Alice in a wooden chair and pushed her head down to her knees for a few moments.

"No, no, I have no wish to be a nuisance," objected Alice, struggling up. "I am perfectly well. I have driven rather a long way this morning, for me that is to say, and I am somewhat tired. There is no call for any anxiety, I assure you. All I need to know is how to get to this school -" She found her diary at last and riffled through to where she had made a note of the address. "I have to see a Mrs. Lestrange, a teacher of English there. Unless I arrive during the lunch hour it may be difficult for me to see her. What is the time please? I omitted to put my watch on this morning. So foolish. I do trust I am not already too late."

Audrey had found her a glass of water. "It's not quite half past twelve. Now, are you sure you're all right? If you've driven a long way since breakfast, maybe you need something to eat. I know I flag when I'm hungry."

"That is exactly what the nice lorry driver said." Alice smiled wanly. "They have a mandatory stop for refreshment, he told me."

"There's a little cafe round the corner, modest, but quite clean," suggested Audrey, hovering maternally. "Meanwhile, can I get you a cup of tea?"

"Truly, I must not take advantage of your kindness. All I require is directions to the school."

Audrey considered. "I'm afraid I don't know where it is," she confessed. "Reg!" she called into the interior. "Can you lay your hands on an A to Z? There's a lady here wants directions to a school." She turned to Alice. "Which school was it again?" She left her there on the chair while she made a pot of tea and Reg hunted about in the back room, finally appearing in triumph with the guide book. Alice gratefully accepted her tea, wrinkled her nose at its strength and sweetness but drank it politely.

"Come on, drink up," encouraged Audrey. "The sugar will do you good. I'm sure what you really need is something to eat," she added.

Reg explained the route, pointing it out on the map; round the one way system, right and right again, three quarters of the way round the roundabout (not that one again, prayed Alice silently) under the arches, over the... He became aware of Alice's eyes glazing over.

"Are you sure you're fit to drive?" he pressed her kindly.

She gave herself a little shake and smiled. "Oh yes, thank you so much. The tea is a wonderful pick-me-up. Especially the sugar, I am sure. But could you perhaps explain the way again for me? It appears to be extremely complicated; I am not a very experienced navigator I fear."

Reg drew her a beautiful plan, marked up with clear arrows and flagged with the names to look out for marked up in sharp capitals, which she took reverently, like an icon or a talisman, and the two Samaritans went outside with her to point the way through the maze of mean streets back to that formidable roundabout.

"But do stop at that cafe first," urged Audrey.

She and Reg watched the little car out of sight. "I bet she won't," she said to him. "I do feel worried about that little soul, Reg," she confided. "I'm sure she ought not to be on the road. And I'm sure too that she has some serious trouble that is driving her beyond her strength. There was no way she was going to talk to us about it though. Goodness knows what may happen."

"Audrey, my dear," said Reg, courteously escorting her back to the office. "It is not your responsibility. Relax."

By this time Alice was past worrying about any effect she might be having on fellow road users. If she felt the need to refer to Reg's instructions, which she did at almost every junction, she would stop in the near lane for the purpose, yellow lines or clearways notwithstanding. Only thus did she feel confident - if that was the word - of staying on the right course. Once she caught sight of a sign proclaiming the Sixth Form College off to the left (or did that mean the right?) and slowed to a crawl again while she considered and rejected it. It was not there that Mrs. Lestrange had been Stephen's teacher; she had not taught him beyond matric, or school cert, or whatever it was called nowadays. So she went on. She appeared to be going to Uttoxeter and Derby after all, but there it was, she followed Reg's plan like holy writ and at last found herself turning in at the school gates, up its drive, parking in front of its long imposing bulk and entering the foyer. Shown to a seat by a reception clerk, she waited while shadowy figures crossed and recrossed, met and parted all round her, without their making the slightest impression on her mind.

Someone stopped in front of her. A voice spoke.

"I'm Betty Lestrange. What can I do for you?"

Alice tried to draw her into focus. She saw two brown eyes, mottled and shining like pebbles in the bottom of a rock pool, or fat, shut-up sea anemones in a tangle of seaweed, no, in a mass of hair; was she drowning, poor thing? Or was it perhaps she herself?

Betty Lestrange straightened up. "I haven't got a lot of time," she said, trying not to look as harassed as she felt. "I'm almost due for a class." And the worst one of my week, as she did not say.

Alice pulled herself together and apologised. "Of course," she said, "you can have no idea who I am, as you have been in correspondence not with me but with Mr. Ratcliffe. Of Weston-super-Mare -"

"Stephen Venables' friend!" Mrs. Lestrange forgot her class. "Oh yes, what a shocking thing! I was so very grieved. You were a friend of his too?"

"Indeed I was." Alice's eyes prickled. "I had become extremely fond of him."

"As had I," murmured his teacher, mournfully. "How can I...?"

"If you would be so kind - I -"

"You don't look well, Miss Fairbairn, if I may say so. Can I arrange to get you anything?"

"Thank you, no. People are all so good. If you would just let me have Stephen's home address? Mr. Ratcliffe did write to ask you for it, but I am sorry to say I was in too much of a hurry to get away this morning to wait for its arrival."

"A hurry?"

"Yes. I am very anxious to see his mother, poor woman."

"I understand." The address was produced and scribbled, together with another little street plan, on the back of the one so meticulously drawn by Reg the Samaritan. "If you're sure you want to get straight off? Very well. Good luck. I'm Betty, by the way.

Please keep in touch."

"Goodbye, Betty, and many thanks." Alice got to her feet and stumbled uncertainly towards the door. Betty Lestrange watched her a moment with troubled eyes, then turned and hared along the corridor, five minutes late for her D stream class, who would not be containing themselves in patience.

The Mini finally passed out at the corner of Hardwick Street and Alice was obliged to get out and walk. For the first time in forty years she forgot to lock the car door. Peering doggedly at such street numbers as survived, she found and knocked at number thirty two. The door opened.

"Yes?"

"I am Miss Fairbairn," said Alice to the apparition fluctuating in the doorway before her.

"So? Who she?"

"I've come about Stephen."

"Stephen? You know where -" His mother's voice was a shriek. But she never finished her frantic question because Alice had pitched full length across her doorsill.

Peter dared not stop for lunch, though he was obliged to for what the Yanks, he recalled wryly, called a 'comfort stop'. He bought himself a sandwich while he was about it and ate it later in a layby as he studied the town plan in the back of his road atlas. Had he only known it, he was parked within yards of where Alice had encountered her friendly lorry driver. The A500 was going to be his best bet and he wasted no time on it. Following an educated guess he turned off at the Meir junction and before long spotted what he sought, a post office. The first reasonable parking space was fifty yards beyond it but, though the driving had made him terribly stiff, he somehow forced himself to get going on his sticks. The post office had something of the air of being under siege; its bare interior stripped for action, it housed two apathetic, down-at-heel queues. Peter was disinclined to wait, so, spotting someone, clearly the boss, moving between the women assistants behind the reinforced glass windows, in the most pleasant and natural way he caught the man's eye and signalled him. In a moment, bypassing the queues with easy charm, he had the man's full attention at a newly opened window.

"Don't let me hold things up. I believe I am in the neighbourhood of Hardwick Street? Yes? A lucky shot - I'm a stranger to the area. Would you please direct me? Excellent."

"Not the most salubrious of neighbourhoods," confided the postmaster, unfolding a town plan on the counter between them. He spoke very low, with a covert glance at the queues of folk gazing dispassionately at them. "Not meaning any offence to the good people unfortunate enough to be living there, but -" he eyed Peter up and down, too old, he judged, to have professional business in that street, but what other reason could he have? - "are you sure you have the correct address?"

Peter was quite sure. He thanked the postmaster and made his laborious way back to the car, more anxious for his rash little friend than ever. He followed the directions he had been given into a labyrinth of streets that screamed of brave municipal attempts to provide a decent environment for working people; a few trees, little front gardens, some of which had tiny lawns and flower beds in shrunken winter dress, others which were rank with weeds and cluttered with broken toys, sodden cardboard boxes and mattresses, twisted washing machines and supermarket trolleys. Just before the turn into Hardwick Street he saw what he was certain was Alice's car. That hat on the back window ledge, he had seen her wear it. Not many people wore hats these days, a charming idiosyncracy of hers. The car was untenanted. She must have walked the last few yards for some reason. He slipped into gear again and pulled round the corner into Hardwick Street. Some of the windows here were boarded up, he observed with mounting disquiet, and doors crisscrossed with timber where they had been kicked in, a clear demonstration of what the postmaster had meant. Number thirty two was in better shape than most.

He manoeuvred his way up the path and knocked.

WPC Shepherd had lunched as healthily as possible on smoked mackerel salad at the last service station south of Stoke, hesitated over a dessert and settled for coffee. She tidied up in the Ladies, had a good stretch and walked briskly back to her blue-chequered car. She was singing to herself, 'Isn't it a lovely day', a song her mother used to sing to her when she was little. Even Hardwick Street wouldn't look such a dump on a day like this.

Chapter Seventeen

Alice revived to find herself confronted by the distraught face of Stephen's mother - the same soft grey eyes, the same expressive mouth - who had deposited her into the hollowed corner of a large settee that had taken hard punishment. Kneeling beside it, she was now offering her a glass of water with one hand and fanning her with the other, anchoring herself meanwhile by her elbows on the settee arm between them.

"Thank God," the woman said as Alice sipped from the glass. "Passed right out you did. You OK now? Want a cup of tea?"

Alice smiled tremulously. "If you are having one, yes, please, Mrs. - er - Mrs.? Not Venables any more, I presume."

"No, not for ages. Blackmore, Gloria Blackmore."

"Would it be very impolite of me to beg one of those bananas, Mrs. Blackmore?" There was a bunch of them spilling out of an Asda bag on a chair. "I think my wretched weakness may be due to hunger in point of fact, a sensation I am not familiar with. So very silly of me. I do apologise. Goodness gracious, yes."

"Sure, sure." Gloria jumped up to get her one. "But you did say 'Stephen', didn't you? I didn't make that up? For God's sake, tell me." She was on her knees beside Alice again. "Going off like that, naughty, naughty boy. I never even knew if he got to college all right or anything. Where did he get to? He didn't know you, did he? How do you -? Where did you run into him?"

"It was in Weston-super-Mare that I met him, poor boy."

"What the devil was he doing there then? We don't know anyone in that place, only went on a trip once, so...?"

"I have no idea why he came there. I was hoping to find out from you. He was on the streets when I first saw him."

"What do you mean?"

"He was living - on - the - streets, Mrs. Blackmore."

"What? Begging? Oh my God, Stephen, like you see on the telly? Homeless kids?"

"Exactly, poor child."

Stephen's mother sat back on her heels, hands behind her head pushing it down between the elbows with which she still clutched the settee arm. "How could he do this to me?" she wailed. "Naughty, naughty boy, he doesn't need, he could at least have written - I would have sent him -"

"My dear, he did write, twice. We gave him stationery and stamps and we actually watched him post the letters. Did you not receive them?"

Gloria's face reappeared, white with shocked disbelief. "But I never - Bugger, there's Wayne back!"

The sound of the kitchen door opening and closing silenced them. Alice looked round for somewhere to put her banana skin and finally, fastidiously, laid it on top of one of its slimy brown elder brothers on the further arm of the settee.

"Glore," came a deep voice from the kitchen. Someone was moving about out there, putting things down, opening and shutting the fridge. "You got someone in there? Or you been talking to yourself?" He appeared in the doorway, an opened can of beer in his hand, standing poised and tall, the dwindling October sun streaming in on him from the window behind; a strong handsome face, eyes like coals beneath distinctive black eyebrows, lips parted in arrested speech, revealingly strikingly white teeth.

"You," he said softly.

Startled by the look on Alice's face, his wife looked enquiringly over her shoulder at him, but he was intent upon the old woman.

"How come?" Gloria asked uncertainly, looking from the one to the other. "You look like you've met before."

"Oh yes." Alice was trapped in the depths of her seat, but centred and alert at last. "We've met. Now I know what your husband was looking for when he burgled my flat, Mrs. Blackmore. He was looking for your son."

"I never found him though," he said, with deadly pleasantness, his eyes never leaving hers. "Not a sign of him."

"Oh yes" - and she was as steady as an old tree stump now - "I think you found him."

He turned back into the kitchen where they could hear him rummaging about in drawers.

"You bastard," said his wife, climbing to her feet, "you bloody fucking bastard, you knew where he was, you stole his letters, my letters you knew I was killing myself every day to get, you went looking for him without ever telling me. You knew where he was and you never told me."

"Shut it, Glore," he said. "I got to think."

She went to him and slid her arms round his waist, rubbing her head into the hollow below his shoulder. "Let's go and fetch him, love, let bygones be bygones. It'll be all right. It will. He'll've learnt his lesson. We can make it all right between us all. If we only make the effort."

Alice gave up the struggle to release herself from the unsprung settee's embrace. "Mrs. Blackmore -" It was hard not to weep. "Mrs. Blackmore, I am afraid you have not understood. I have been trying to break it to you - oh dear, I am making such a mess of things - you see, when I arrived I had no idea you had not been told. My dear, I am so very sorry to have to tell you that your son is dead."

"Dead?" Gloria stood back and looked first at her husband and then at Alice. "No way. He's only seventeen. And he's so clever. Wayne, tell her." She gave a shrill laugh. "He ran away, that's what happened."

"Yes. But now he is dead," said Alice with bursting heart. "Your husband could have told you that."

Gloria stared first at her and then at him. "But he isn't dead, is he, Wayne? You hadn't heard that, Wayne had you? You would've told me, wouldn't you, if he was dead. Maybe you did know where he had run off to, OK, but you never had any idea he was dead, did you? Did you?"

"No, I didn't know that." His voice was steady. He was still watching Alice.

"Oh, yes, Mr. Blackmore, you did. He went to Weston with the police, Mrs. Blackmore. They fetched him down to identify the body, while you were on your touring holiday."

105

"What? What touring holiday? I should be so lucky! That what you told them, Wayne? So it's true then? And you did know? And you didn't tell me, you hid it from me. Oh my God -"

"Shut up, the both of you. Glore, bring me them tights off the airer." She was staring at him again, stock still. "Move!" He launched a savage kick that doubled her up. "Now. The tights."

She complied, bent over, shielding her eyes.

"I'm going upstairs for something. You can get on with tying old Mother Riley up. - What's that? With the tights, headcase, what you think I want them for? Hands and feet, and make it bloody tight."

"Wayne, why? She's an old lady."

"Shut it, I said." Still low and even, his tone was venomous. "She's a nosey old fucker. I don't trust her. Do it. Now. I've got ears and I'm quick, you know that." He went upstairs.

Moving softly, placatorily, wincing still with pain from the kick in her pubis, Gloria tied Alice's wrists together and then her ankles. She whispered apologetically, defensively. "I'm sorry, I really am. I have to, you see. You do see that? And it would be best for you not to struggle."

Alice whispered too and was answered in mute gestures. "Are you afraid of him?" Gloria's eyes widened. "This is not the first time he has hurt you like that then?" Gloria closed in on herself, wincing. "Did he hurt Stephen? Is that why he ran away?" A painful shrug. "Or because he saw you being hurt and was powerless to stop it?" A tear rolled. Alice whispered, so gently, "He said 'my poor mum'. That is what he said to me, 'My poor mum', his last words on this earth." With a deep sob, Gloria's head sank to her knees. "Why do you stay with him, that man?" The last knot half-tied in her hands, Gloria raised her head and looked round the room at the litter of toys, colouring books, a skateboard against the wall behind the door. "Oh, I see, you have other children. But do you not want to take them away from this violence too?"

Alice had to strain to hear the strangled reply, "They're his children, this lot, aren't they. - Is that too tight? I don't want to hurt you."

"What do you think he intends to do?"

"God knows what he's got in his mind. But he'll get over

it and see sense if we're quiet. That's where my Stephen made his error. I kept telling him. He would stand up to him and make him look a fool. That's what he can't stand, being made to look a fool. - What did my boy die of? Please tell me. You were there, weren't you. It should of been me there."

Wayne came down the stairs.

"Now," he said to Alice, "How d'you get here? Car?"

She nodded.

"There's nothing outside. Where is it then?"

"Round the corner. I ran out of petrol I fear."

"You what? Bloody hell - that's gone out of touch then."

There was a knock at the door. Gloria gave him an enquiring look. He silenced them both with a brusque gesture.

"Get down," he mouthed. "Cover her up with that washing Glore, and stay out of sight of that window."

She did. The only sounds in the room were made by their breathing and Alice's digestive tract.

Again a knock. Then they heard the click of the letter box spring.

"I believe you have a Miss Fairbairn there." Peter's voice. Alice's heart leapt. Thank goodness you have come, she thought. And rapidly countermanded the idea, realising that he too was now at risk.

"Mr. Blackmore, or Mrs. Blackmore, if you are there, please open the door. Miss Fairbairn was intending to call on you and I see her car is close by, so..."

"Glore," whispered Wayne between those shining teeth, "take a look - careful, mind."

With a fearful glance at him she crept to the window and peered through the corner of the curtain. "It's an old bloke, on sticks."

"Christ, what is this? An old folks treat?"

"Otherwise," continued Peter through the letter box, "since I am concerned for the lady's safety, I shall be obliged to enlist the aid of the police."

"Better let him in Glore. Keep your trap shut until you've got him in here and the door's shut. Or old Mother Riley's dead. OK?"

With a pleading glance at Alice, she went.

"Forgive the intrusion, Mrs. Blackmore," Peter began, as he laboured down the hall and into the living room. "Ah, good afternoon, Mr. Blackmore, I thought Miss Fairbairn..." His voice trailed away as he realised what had only just come home to the two women, that it was a hand gun that Blackmore held on the settee arm, nonchalantly pointed at Alice's head.

"Ah," said Peter, lowering himself into the chair to which Gloria had led him.

"Get a couple more tights, Glore. He'll need tying up too."

"There's only one pair left there, Wayne. You don't want me to use the ones I've got on, do you? His hands'll be enough, surely love, he's a cripple. What are you going to do, love?" she whimpered, as she tied Peter's wrists, her eyes eloquent with apologies, his eyes anxiously on his rash little friend, who was still batting with her bound hands to rid herself of the dirty laundry smothering her face, the hand gun still so close to her white head. "Aren't you going a bit far? And the boys'll be home in a minute."

"Right. You let 'em in here and you're dead as well as old Mother Riley. Tell 'em to go to Amy's. It won't be the first time. Got it?"

"What children do you have?" asked Alice, trying to lighten the tension. She had decided that the gun, which she could just see out of the corner of her eye, was exactly like the one belonging to the little boy she so enjoyed watching at play in Grove Park and was therefore nothing to be afraid of.

Gloria appealed mutely to her husband before answering. "There's Lee. He's nine. And Jason, seven. Stephen was ever so good with them. They love him dearly - Miss Fairhead, he isn't really dead, is he? Tell me he isn't dead, Miss Fairhead."

"Shut up," hissed Wayne, through gritted teeth. "I got to think. You -" He shifted the gun to point at Peter. "You got a car out there?"

"Of course."

"How much petrol in it? She!" He aimed the gun at Alice once more. "She ran out."

"I must have over a hundred miles in the tank. I must

warn you, however, if you're thinking of hi-jacking it, the controls are adapted for my disability."

"No worries. You'll be driving."

"Moreover, the interior is adapted to take my wheelchair, so I can only take one passenger."

"We'll chuck out the wheelchair and put 'em on the floor. Better that way anyway - hide 'em under a rug or something. - How long before school's out?"

Gloria peeked through into the kitchen at the clock. "Ten minutes."

"OK, we'll go. I've put two bags of our stuff at the foot of the stairs, Glore. You take those. Untie the old fucker's feet, she's got to walk. You-" - he jerked a shoulder at Peter - "get up. We're leaving. Bloody hell, Glore, give him a heave, he's fucking useless. Anyone out of line and the old girl's dead, right? No -"

"What about the boys, love?"

"They'll go to Amy's, they're not stupid - even if they are mine," he added, viciously.

There was a brisk knock at the door. They stopped in midstep.

"Shit!" he hissed under his breath. "I don't believe this! Glore?"

She crept to the spy curtain.

The knock was repeated, then a voice came through the letterbox. "Hallo, Mr. Blackmore? You at home? It's WPC Shepherd from Weston-super-Mare, remember me?"

"Holy shit!" The whisper was intense. "Get down, Glore."

"You got visitors in there? There's two cars out here from our patch."

"Wayne," wailed Gloria, "what do you think you're doing? That's the police. And the kids'll be here in a minute. What are we doing about the kids?"

"Is that Mrs. Blackmore I can hear in there?" called Sandra through the letterbox. "That's good. I did particularly want to see you."

"Get down, Glore. I mean it."

"Wayne, what is it? What's eating you? I know you and

Stephen never got on, but now he's dead, Wayne..."

"Bloody superior little bastard," her husband muttered, his lip curling in a way so reminiscent of the arrogant expression that had much distressed her at its rare fleeting appearances on Stephen's face that Alice caught her breath. With a flash of insight she felt the pain of the relationship between this proud, bitter, unsuccessful man (she cast an involuntary glance at the squalor round them) and the brilliant angry boy who had 'stood up to him' and 'made him look a fool', the boy whom Wayne's own children had 'loved dearly' because he was 'so good with them', better than their short-tempered father, perhaps. She gazed with a rush of compassion at the man who was holding a gun to her head.

"Alice," said Peter, watching her face, "if we both come through this adventure alive, will you marry me?"

She wasn't sure she had heard aright. Blinking, she slowly turned her head towards him, her face transfigured by awed disbelief.

"Shut it," said Wayne savagely, rescuing her from the need of the moment. "What's that police cow doing, Glore? Have a see through the letterbox."

"She's gone to her car. She's talking on her mobile. What's she want, Wayne? You do know her, from when he died, like the old lady said, don't you? She did say, didn't she - Christ! You did see him, didn't you! When was it? When you said you had those jobs away? Driving jobs, temporary? I thought they smelt a bit, you were so jumpy. And I never saw any money off them. I thought, you cheapskate. That was weeks ago, months even. You did see him. And you never told me. You stole his letters. His letters to me. Why, Wayne? Why?"

They heard the sirens of another police car approaching at speed. It stopped outside.

"What they doing Glore?" Wayne's whole body was rigid with the effort of control.

"There's one chap coming to the door with the woman cop. Looks like the other one's going round the back. What's going on Wayne? What do the Bill want? Untie these people, there's a good lad, or let me. We can't have the cops coming in with them like that, we'd be nicked for sure. Go on, untie them. If I ask them to forget all about it for Stephen's sake they will, I'm sure they will, they were his friends. Here, you and that woman cop know each other - let her in and we'll explain -"

"Shut it!" The cords in his neck were quivering. "You're stopping me thinking."

"Open up, Blackmore," called a man's voice. "We know you're in there. We just want a word, that's all. Tell you the latest news about your stepson."

"See?" cried Gloria, elated. "Told you! Now shall I open the door?"

"Shut your face, you stupid cow. I told you, get away from that door."

"Come on, Blackmore," called the policeman heartily. "You want us to think something's up?"

"Clear off if you don't want to get hurt!" shouted Wayne.

"Don't play silly buggers, man."

Wayne put a shot straight through the door. The bullet passed between Sandra and the local man, smacked into a gatepost and fell crumpled and exhausted in the road.

Chapter Eighteen

"Now what?" asked Sandra of the officer whose patrol car had answered her request for backup. She was very quiet and white. There was the bullet in the road. There was the hole in the door. There was no sound from within.

"Back off and report," he replied, hardly above his breath, suiting action to the word. "Never met this sort of thing before? That's all right, some of us have. Take your car up the corner, out of the line of fire. Here comes Charlie - reverse down the junction, Chas, ditto, and then call in. Then we get all the neighbours out and clear the area. Got it?"

Sandra fielded a chattering crowd of little ones who at that moment came leaping and caterwauling homeward, about to turn into the back alleys of Hardwick Street. This was a job she could do and do well. "Want a look at my cop car?" she called and they had their Pied Piper. The mothers who had met them from school came over, curious, indignant, truculent, melted first by Sandra's sweet-smiling manner, reluctantly persuaded in the end to go with their children to relatives, friends, anywhere out of the danger zone.

"Shooting!" they said, wondering, to each other. "Well, the fuzz are no strangers round here, but shooting! Well!"

At last only two children were left. "What's your names then?" asked Sandra.

"I'm Jason. Stephen says - that's our brother, see, he's gone away to college now, but I won't half be glad when he gets back, he's really really wicked - he says I'm the boss of the Argonauts and I've got this great boat" -

"Ship," put in his brother.

"All right, ship, called the Argo, but he made it all himself, him and his friends, I mean me, and it's got oars as well as sails and I get to sail through millions of perils and get the golden fleece in the end."

"And I'm Lee, and Stephen says I can choose to be Laurie Lee and write books and poetry and stuff like Stephen does or I can be a man who invents rifles for the American army if I'd rather, or even be a Nobel scientist, it's up to me. I'm going to wait and see. He says, 'Good lad, that's the way.' "

"I wish Stephen would come back," said Jason, wistfully. "He has awful fights with our Dad, but I don't care. It's Dad's fault. Only he better not hit Stephen, that's all."

"Yeah, it'll be good when Stephen gets home," said Lee, mourning, "he's dead great, is Stephen."

"Aren't you getting our Mum to come for us? We only live over there."

"She's on nights this month, she'll be home."

"She's a bit busy just now," said Sandra, succeeding in finding a smile from somewhere. That 'dead great' was choking her. "She'll be along soon I guess. Want a go of my blue lights?"

Inside the house the shocked silence was long.

"I can't believe you just did that," said Gloria at last. "What's it all about love?"

Watching this battered woman slink submissively up to her husband, her posture still awkwardly accommodating her bruise, and slide her arms round his waist again, Alice felt the hairs stirring at the back of her neck. Could she herself ever have been so debased, so subservient to a man as that? Daddy had never struck her, it was inconceivable. But then he had never needed to, she had never questioned his word (except in her often rebellious thoughts.) 'Needed to'? Whatever was she thinking? How could a kick like that ever be considered 'necessary'? It had been a dreadful shock to her. That the gun was after all genuine had also been a severe shock. She turned her head and met Peter's eye. He winked at her. She repaid his grin with a brave little smile. There was no end to the way people surprised one, she reflected, her attention once more focussed on the Blackmores. He was positioned in the doorway, whence he had a clear view of the front door as well as of the whole of the room, his head slightly bent under the lintel, his shoulders supported against the jamb. He reminded Alice of the pictures of Atlas holding up the world on the cover of a long-ago school book about the Greek myths. What was the burden this man carried? Guilt? Jealousy? Failure? All three?

The phone rang. Gloria's automatic movement towards it was arrested by a flick of her husband's left hand. It rang for a long time unanswered, as the tension mounted in the silence. Then it stopped.

"What can you see from the window, Glore?"

She peered through the curtain. "Street's empty. Nothing's happening. No kids out. Nothing. It's weird, Wayne, frightening."

"You know," said Peter, offhand, "I don't know about the rest of you, but I'm an old man and I shall very shortly have to take a trip to the little boys' room."

"Shut it," said Wayne. "Nobody's taking any trips till we all go together."

"Dear me," said Peter pleasantly, "that doesn't sound like a very nice party to me. There are ladies present."

Alice looked at him in amazement, worked out what he had meant and turned her head away, blushing furiously. Then she stole another look at him and found refuge in laughter. They both laughed.

"God almighty!" shouted Wayne, out of control for a moment. "What is this? A nuthouse?"

"I am sorry," apologised Alice, in genuine contrition. "That was hardly considerate of us when you are so upset. No indeed." Doubled up in the broken-springed seat, her feet, so recently unbound, sticking out in front of her like a doll's, she was becoming acutely uncomfortable. Both her feet had gone to sleep. Moreover, she was concerned about Peter's predicament. How long would it be, she wondered, after all that tea, before she herself was in trouble. Oh dear - the wish was in this case father to the urge! Oh dear, the indelicacy of advancing years!

The phone rang again.

"You'll have to talk to them sometime, Mr. Blackmore," Peter pointed out. "We can't all stay like this for ever."

"How can I work out what to say with this fucking row

going on? Shut your trap, will you, and let me think! Shut the bloody thing up Glore."

She took the phone off the hook and left it dangling.

"What is it they want, Wayne?" she pleaded, going to him and sliding her arms round his waist again. "Is it about Stephen? How did he die, Wayne? You know, don't you. You saw him dead, my darling boy, my lovely, clever Stephen, you must have seen him. She said, her over there, she said you 'identified the body' - oh what a thing to call him, 'the body', like that. - But you didn't love him, did you, not ever, even when he was only little and his dad just dead -"

"I tried," said Wayne, low, between his teeth.

His words broke like boulders from a dam, in distinct grinding shifts. "I tried. He'd cry. So I'd cuddle him. And he went all stiff on me. Little bugger. I'd kiss him. He'd turn his head away. As far as ever he could stretch his neck. Like I smelt or something."

"Wayne, he was only a baby. He was missing his dad. He wasn't three when you moved in. You can't expect a baby -"

The words came crashing out now like a thunder of waters. "I gave him a toy, cost me a bomb, he threw it out - I tried to feed him, he spit stuff all over me - everything he wanted I gave him if I could - he wanted books, I bought him books - and he throws them on the floor and looks at me like I was dirt. And him only a snotty kid -"

"Wayne, you didn't get him books, you got him the Beano! What's the good of the Beano to a boy like that?"

"There you go - that's it - I didn't know no better did I? I wasn't never good enough, was I? He always made that bloody clear! And so did you! What's the good of a man like me with no bits of paper to back me? I couldn't never be father to that fucking genius, that angel out of heaven. Never mind it was me put the roof over his head and the food in his mouth and worked my butt off so he could get educated and wave those bits of paper in my face. So what if I lost my job? I got another. Jobs haven't been easy for no-one, you know that, not round here, and now I'm knocking fifty. It ain't going to get better. But I've bloody tried. And I've kept straight, for you and the boys - oh yeah, I know you thought it was me the getaway driver those times, no faith in me, I know that -

fucking bloody hell, it was hard, but I tried. I didn't never give in. And I never took nothing out of my money but what you give me. But I wasn't nobody's golden boy, not with him around. I thought when he went off I'd get a bit of respect and peace in my own house, but no, it's worse than ever, Stephen, Stephen, the place is fuller of Stephen than ever when he isn't even here! I'm here - this is me - can't you see me? Can't you hear me? Gone deaf or something? Can't you hear nothing but Stephen? Not only you but the boys too, my own kids -"

Tears snailed down Alice's cheeks and into the corners of her mouth.

"I didn't know you hated him like that," said Gloria slowly. "You never talked so much in your whole life." She stopped, her chest suddenly caved in, her eyes wide. "Christ, Wayne, how did he die? He was killed Wayne, wasn't he. Was it you killed him? Went down to Weston to find him and killed him there?"

"I never meant to, Glore, honest to God. That wasn't what I went for. I'd got those letters - you was at work when they come, one time you was sleeping - why should he - oh God, I don't know why I hid them - I went to the address he sent and it was the old woman's place but he wasn't there. So I hung about for hours watching it, back and front, keeping out of sight. It was nearly dark when he come along that path, looking up at her windows. I tried to talk to him, Glore, tell him how it was even worse at home with him gone walkabout. And all he wanted off me was those fucking exam results. Would he listen, just for one fucking moment, to what mattered to me, would he hell - no, fuck me, fuck my family, fuck me coming down all that way hitching down just to get things sorted between us, no, none of that mattered, only his blasted bits of paper - Glore, you listening to me? - So I was so mad I tore the letter up, the letter they sent him, and threw it in the sea."

Just the way Rob tore up and threw away his poetry, thought Alice, weeping.

"Was that his exam results?" cried Gloria in horror. "You had his exam results and you wouldn't give them to him? You bastard! You bastard! Those are what he needed to get to Cambridge, if they were good enough."

"They were good enough," said Peter.

Wayne was deaf and blind to everything now but that encounter on the cliff top. "And then he bloody hit me, silly little fucker, so -"

"So you beat him to a pulp," said Peter.

"And threw him over the cliff after his letter," mourned Alice.

Gloria flew at her husband in so unprecedented an onslaught that the gun was knocked out of his hands. She was using her teeth and nails to good effect before he recovered sufficiently from the first shock to grasp her by the wrists, forcing her backwards, twisting his hips to fend off those vicious knees, finding the wall and smashing her head against it.

"Peter!" cried Alice, struggling desperately to free herself from her prison. "He's doing just what he did to Stephen - the wall - she'll be -"

Agonisingly slowly, Peter was reaching with his bound hands for his sticks, stretching for them till he trembled with the strain and toppled headlong into a Lego masterpiece. But he had one of his sticks at last and thrust it between the man's legs, bringing him down heavily on his back.

"Alice! The gun!" he urged, but Gloria, released, beat her to it. By the time Wayne, gasping and wheezing, was on his feet, she was aiming it steadily at him, her back braced against the kitchen door.

"Stupid cow, you can't," he said, bearing down on her. He was already grabbing for her when she shot him full in the face.

Alice, free at last, stumbled on numb feet to the telephone, reaching it just as her ankles gave way and pitched her too on to the floor.

*

"Tell you what," said Rob next day to his father, who was bringing him home in triumph from the juvenile detention centre where he had been held on remand, "that old woman's a hero. We'd'a' never got off but for her and that's a fact."

"You're right there, son, no messing. And let that be a lesson to you, stick by your friends, like she done, no matter what, and never tell no lies. Got it?"

Rob gave his father a long quizzical look. "Got it," he said.

*

"Full marks to your hunch then, Sand," observed Sergeant Hopsack as they cleared up the Weston incident room. "Turns out to be a domestic nine times out of ten of course."

"You know, Sarge," said Sandra slowly, her perfect face serious, pensive even, "it's a funny thing, considering I never met this young man Venables to speak of, only for seeing him by Boots, I feel, now, like he was a friend, know what I mean, I'm really cut up about him. You know who's going to miss him most? Go on, guess. His kid brothers." She told him what they had said, then, smiling the tenderest, most sorrowful smile, "It's enough to break your heart," she said.

Look like that much more, you'll break mine, thought Sergeant Hopsack, slamming the last drawer shut.

*

The police undertook to bring Alice's Mini back to Weston-super-Mare. Peter took her home, driving down the motorways with dreamlike ease.

"What will happen to Stephen's beloved mother, his 'poor mum'?" she asked, after a long silence.

"My guess is a manslaughter charge," he replied, "and with our evidence and that of the hospital, not to mention what the police may well have heard when the phone was off the hook, leaving the line to them open, it would be surprising if she didn't get off entirely with a plea of self defence."

"Stephen was right to be afraid for her."

"A tragic family, in the true Greek sense. Poor wretched woman."

"Poor man, too," sighed Alice.

"Poor unhappy boy" and "Poor poor Stephen" they said together. Tears ran silently on to her collar.

"Alice" he said, after another long pause - they were swinging steadily in and out of the outside lane, the Malverns on their right standing purple against the gold of the evening sky - "you never answered my question."

"What question?" But little shivers were running down

her back.

"In however decrepit a state," he went on, "we have survived this adventure. Will you marry me?"

"Peter," she said, "that question was asked at a very heightened moment. I would never dream of holding you to it."

He laughed. "I shall understand if you prefer your independence to tying yourself to this old hulk."

"Oh Peter, you must not think that! But after so many years of spinsterhood, I find the prospect of marriage unbelievable, truly beyond imagination."

"Well, take your time. Though at our age that is a commodity we have in short supply."

"Meanwhile, dear Peter, may we be the best of friends?"

They were thoughtful again for a long while.

Then she spoke. "Peter, do you think it would be a good idea if I were to acquire a television set?"

*